Jenny Diski was born in 1947. She is the author of eight novels, a collection of short stories and a book of essays as well as a highly acclaimed memoir, *Skating to Antarctica*. She is also the *Mail of Sunday*'s radio critic and a regular contributor to the *London Review of Books*. She lives in Cambridge.

Also by Jenny Diski

Novels

Nothing Natural
Rainforest
Like Mother
Then Again
Happily Ever After
Monkey's Uncle
The Dream Mistress

Short stories

The Vanishing Princess

Essays

Don't

Memoir

Skating to Antartica

ONLY HUMAN

A Comedy

Jenny Diski

A *Virago* Book

Published by Virago Press 2001
First published by Virago Press 2000

Copyright © Jenny Diski 2000

The moral right of the author has been asserted

A CIP catalogue record for this book
is available from the British Library

ISBN 1 86049 914 7

Typeset in Bembo by M Rules
Printed and bound in Great Britain by
Clays Ltd, St Ives plc

Virago Press
A Division of
Little, Brown and Company (UK)
Brettenham House
Lancaster Place
London WC2E 7EN

For Frances Coady
with love and thanks

ENDINGS

And at the end she is lachrymose.

She lies propped up with cushions on a thin mattress, barely covered with a light cloth, open-eyed, seeing nothing, waiting, it seems. She is ancient, so full of years that they pool for want of space in pockets of her loose flesh, dragging it earthwards, decade-heavy pouches drooping under her eyes, at her jaw, neck, her slack breasts, hanging belly, limp thighs; substanceless sacks but weighted with the years her slight frame can no longer support under the relentless pressure of gravity. Intermittently, she weeps: silently without any sudden surge of passion or obvious cause, as if the tears were welled already, brim full behind her shrunken eyes, and leak like spillage over the lids whose muscles are not strong enough to dam them up. Eyes sunken, verging towards colourlessness, rims margined red without lashes. When she speaks, beginning to answer the questions her concerned visitors put to her, she does so also without passion in a cracked, whispered monotone, then stops to allow the tears to course down the deep folds and crazes in her cheeks. Sometimes she dabs them away with a cloth, sometimes she leaves them to drip and drench the small pillow under her head. The tears stop as abruptly as they start, and then she looks up at her questioner with a finished expression, as if her answer had been fully completed by the interrupting tears. What she conveys more than anything is bafflement. Her weeping, the manner of it, lacks a direct cause, is unattached to a single thought, a particular regret. These are tears that come of their own accord, like breath, interrupting speech, thought, and regret.

We are there to sit with her in her final hours, and to honour her for her long life, for her achievements. She is a great, the very greatest of old ladies. Now she is as old as it is possible to get and we are hungry for her conclusions. We want the wisdom she must have gained through such a lengthy life so full of incident. We do not want her to die without telling what at last she knows, without passing on what she has understood from it all.

One of us leans forward with the question that must be asked. 'When you look back . . .'

She stares at her questioner for a second, trying to focus on the mouth as if the words it had spoken clustered around its lips and with an effort she might arrange them into sense, but then, giving up, her eyes wander. When she returns to the face, it is smiling warmly at her, conveying appreciation and encouragement, willing her memory into speech. But when you look carefully, you see her eyes are glazed, not reaching the affirmative face at all.

'. . . back over your life – the extraordinary events you've lived through, the people, the changes, the love, the loss, the influence you've had – what stands out for you as the central thread?'

We wait expectantly. She senses it finally, and her watery eyes stop seeing whatever she was seeing in the middle-distance and return to the present and to her questioner whose question hangs in the air, though it is doubtful if she heard it.

Finally she speaks, though without any apparent reference either to the questioner or the idiotic question.

'I wish I were dead,' she says. And she drops her head and covers her face with her damp cloth as the incidental tears seep from her eyes once again.

The company gasps and then falls into an embarrassed silence. The encouraging smiles die on their faces. Our foolish question hangs frozen in front of us. Slowly, they begin to rise singly and in pairs, and shuffle awkwardly towards the light outside, trying not to show their eagerness to leave.

She still holds the cloth to her face. I squat down beside her.

'I'm sorry,' I say uselessly, and touch my palm against her skeletal shoulder. She looks up slowly, sees me, and places the hand holding the damp cloth over mine. I cover this hand with my own other hand, feeling bone and slack skin, without any padding of flesh in between. There is no sign of her former distress in her face as she searches mine now to see if I am someone familiar. She looks quite composed and yet suddenly the tears come again. When they stop, as abruptly as they started, she looks up and speaks confidentially.

'It was all endings. Always. Endings, starting and ending, but no conclusion.'

She looks directly at me with the hint of a question in her eyes, then lifts one tiny scrawny shoulder in a shrug that is no more than perplexed.

'Nothing else . . .'

Her eyes glaze again, and the pressure of her hand between mine lessens. It is no longer in contact with me, though it continues to lie where it had been placed. Her eyes still look in the direction of my face, unfocused.

Beginnings

Now these are the generations of Terah: Terah begat Abram, Nahor, and Haran; and Haran begat Lot. And Haran died before his father Terah in the land of his nativity, in Ur of the Chaldees.
GENESIS 11:27–28

In the beginning there was love. No. Love comes early, but not quite at the beginning. In the beginning, and in each of our beginnings, there was the precursor to all else: interruption. This is how love starts. But, for a few fleeting moments, life was free simply to be — when it had no need even of innocence. In the beginning, before the interruption, there was life itself.

And it was good ————

———— Damn impertinence! Who dares to speak of the beginning?

Before the beginning, when they were nothing, when nothing was, before the word, before the number and the chapter, before before and after, before he, she and us, before I am that I am, before I will be what I will be — I was, and before I was, I was, when nothing was. And I, in that nothing, of that nothing, a blankness, hovered and haunted the swell of vacuity. In the formlessness and the void, yes, and before it – I was. Before the incoherence, before the unity, before the separation – I was. Before the narrator, before the narrative, before the end implied in the beginning, before the beginning set in motion by the end – I was. Before the story, before the account, before the clarification, before the alibi, before all motivation to explain, before because – *I was*!

And what had been for an eternity, might have remained for an eternity of eternity. And nothing had its say. And it was good.

Yet I made the beginning, in the very beginning. That beginning. I separated and categorised, I called forth kinds, kind after kind. In order, I made order, so that the one could follow the other, and the next could come after the last. I made what came before to sustain what came next. I made a system. I made regulation. From stasis, I made homeostasis. Light from the darkness. Above from below. Dry from wet. Growth: seed seeding, fruits fruiting, seed seeding. Time: dawning, setting, dawning. Animation: fish swimming, birds flying, insects crawling, herds flocking, beasts stalking. Replication: fruit fruiting, seed seeding. Abundance.

All this I spoke into existence. Before the beginning, before the word, before the deed, before the I am, I made all this. And still it was good ⸺⸺

⸺⸺ The beginning of the world (before the beginning, all our beginnings, is none of our concern. A matter of mere curiosity for later, much much later) – the beginning, I say, of the world: an endless day in a garden filled with comfortable warm air riffling across bare skin. The scent of honeysuckle hangs for a second and then drifts past. Bees laden with pollen, making a lurching, overburdened flight back to the hive, hum more and less loudly around her head, coming and going.

But now a silhouette suddenly obscures the sun, looming over, blanked by shadow, and gathers her up into its arms. This is how the beginning of the world – all the languid protracted days of her infancy – was interrupted. The memory is fixed: sharp in the detail apprehended by the senses, yet filled with blank grey shadows of overwhelming power. A small but growing consciousness absorbed the signals of her environment: in it, but more than in it, feeling, sensing, taking in her surroundings in a way that made her distinct from them. Then the great shadow, obstructing the light, overhanging her, throbbing with deep, undulating sound, taking her up, putting her down, quite separate from the environment that merely *was* around her. The shadow – more than her equal, as she was more than the equal of her surroundings by her apprehension of them.

The shadow, or shadows, came booming into her existence and altered her circumstances, changed the world about her, changed her own condition in it from hot to cold, wet to dry, outside to inside, light to dark. Alteration without reason. More than the world, more than herself.

So long ago, but the memory would always stick, of the sweet sharp scent of the honeysuckle, the wafting air on her skin, though, of course, the knowledge that it was honeysuckle smelling and air moving or bees that hummed is from another time. There would be many honeysuckled warm days at memory's disposal to provide the sensual detail with names. The overhanging shadows, however, existed only back then, and sometimes in her dreams. Well, it doesn't matter. The picture of the beginning of the world works whether it has been painted in retrospect or truly exists as a frozen moment of a time before memory had organised itself into meaning.

Out of the overweening anonymous shadows identity eventually emerged. First the fact of their otherness from her, then the knowledge of her otherness from them. Then their otherness from each other. And gradually, the world-altering knowledge that, although she was not them, she was of them and not the honeysuckle, the wind and the bees. The knowledge that the shadows' power to change the nature of her existence, for all her present powerlessness, *was to be hers too*. Possibility entered the beginning of the world, and with it, desire.

Which made her – let us acknowledge the pattern of the world – one with the honeysuckle and bees after all: driven. Hungry for . . . striving after . . . needful. But with the exceptional addition of an increasing self-knowledge that transformed desire into will. At what point, at the beginning of the world, did she stop simply being at the mercy of the omnipotent shadows and begin actively to wish for their intervention, and then, inevitably – let us acknowledge the pattern of the world – to dream of becoming an intervener herself? The longing to become them would have been born. And then the shadows would have become the objects of her desires. Pure life was interrupted by desire. Will? Free will? The birth of love.

Father, mother, others. In a garden, or a courtyard. Obliterating shadows that walled her off from the rest of the world. Surrounded by a wall of love. Later, that would be later, when the words came – the wall of love, the naming of the shadows. She was shown belonging, what was hers by default, and learned attachment. Eventually, when she and the garden were alone together, existing neutrally side by side as they had in the beginning, she understood that the shadows would intervene and intensify her life. Lifting her into the air, where she didn't belong, where she depended on willing arms continuing to hold her safe from the downward pull of the earth. Voices soothing away anxiety. Laughter. If you are cold, we will make you warm; hungry, we will fill you; hurt, we will comfort you; alone, we will enclose you in our wall of love. And soon, she learned to look forward to their intervention in her existence. To look forward. To long for their presence. Being alone in the garden became a lost world of the eternal present of the very beginning. The first loss.

Now there was a future where the shadows might be imagined. With the future, and what it could bring, came the desire that displaced the present. And she was theirs. A beautiful, elegant system: the creation of time and attachment to form the glue that holds us to others. The evolution of love, a.k.a. longing, a.k.a. needing. Striving to belong, aching to be loved.

The father. So large, enclosing, the deep timbre of his voice, an assurance past doubting. No harm could come to her while he blotted out the sun. Yet had she been concerned that harm might come to her before she felt his protection? I doubt it. The protection and the felt need for it came together. What was there to be afraid of before she was told that there was nothing to be afraid of while he was around? The father remained a beloved shadow. The mother – easier to grasp as a reality. The comfort was there as practical improvement. It wasn't her very being, but her doing that kept the child safe at the beginning of the world. It was easier to predict the mother's re-entry into her world. The father was the more magical, the more powerful by virtue of his intermittent and arbitrary interventions. The longing for him was the greatest. He was the least biddable. Uncertainty kept her desire for him intact and her love unconditional. Uncertainty would always wield a special power over her.

That is how it was and is, and we go on to live in the world as we have to. Everyone does. Did and will. It is what all times have in common. It is the way of the world. Yet, though we all live in our times as we must, some have to do it harder. Oh, yes, there are those of us who make more fuss about it than others. Who knows why? Dysfunction, *you* might say. Born like it, I'd say. Starting out with a furrowed brow as if, even swaddled, some little creatures know it isn't going to be easy, well before they know what the *it* they're facing is. This is as much as we are given to stand up against the way of the world ————

———— And then I made my great error. I made sentience. I made self-consciousness. I made *I am*. Whatever anyone might say, I did not know what the consequences would be. Until I made the world, there had been no consequence, only inconsequential eternity. How could I have known? There was no distinction between eternity and the fact of my existence, not until the stirring of consciousness that separated me from it. The first separation.

In my separateness, I toyed with eternity. I divided and rearranged the void and came up with creation. I created. I made a world as self-sufficient as eternity, but more than that, unlike eternity, capable of reproducing itself, and dependent on a creator for its original existence. A marvel. Now I was a maker. Now, distinct from all else, having made all else, I was.

And here, innocence and curiosity got the better of me. I was, but what I was I couldn't say. My existence was defined by all that I had made and was not: eternity, earth, and growing, creeping, flying, flocking, stalking life. I was none of these. I had made these. They lived, creatures of my imagination, without knowledge of what they were, how they had become, who had brought them into being. And who had brought them into being? This question was brought into being also. The first question.

There are no mirrors in eternity. I made a mirror. I imagined a likeness. I created a humankind. I breathed my own self-awareness into the nostrils of the man/woman and set them above all other creation, as I was above all creation, including them. I placed them in a garden, sustained them with all that I had made before. And then, thinking nothing of it, I separated the man/woman into individual entities. And as if that was not enough, I gave them the Word, so that they might name for themselves all that I had created, and so that, being conscious, being self-conscious, they might recognise each other as other and call one another by name. I made two I ams, because in all eternity, there had never been two I ams before.

My mistake. My miscalculation. Just one I am would have been sufficient. The one would have given me the relation I wanted. The human singleton would properly have reflected its creator, and shown me to myself. But how could I know the danger of a doublet of self-awareness? In all existence, such a thing had never been. I was too besotted with my beautiful system of self-replication to consider the possible results of the self-replication of two awarenesses.

Be fruitful and multiply, I told them. Have dominion, I said, meaning, be like me, in order that I might know what I am. But so they should know where we all stood in my scheme of things, I made a prohibition. Just one. Simply so they understood that I was in a position to forbid. That, though they were in my likeness, though they had dominion over the whole earth, it was my earth and they were still my creatures. I invented *don't*.

It went well for a while. I watched as they lived. I saw myself in their existence, separate from their world, eating it, seeding it, enjoying it. I walked with them in the garden. I learned what it was to have the company I had invented for them. I spoke to them, heard the sound of my own voice, and the sound of other voices speaking to me. But self-awareness and even a limited dominion turned out to be a dangerous gift. As I had invented prohibition, so they invented disobedience. My fault, you could say. My single rule was arbitrary, a sign of nothing more than rule itself. The prohibition was merely the map of our relations, the first relations. But it gave them ideas. It gave them the notion of opposition, and I discovered they had an innate flaw in that respect. *Don't* niggled at them until they came up with defiance, and in doing so they became more to each other than they were to me. With that first disobedience, everything changed. They made a new word: they made *us*.

They hid from me. I had to ask, 'Where are you?' I, their creator; they tried to hide from me. With defiance came secrecy. They tried to keep things from me. I knew nothing of secrets. From them I learned of deception: that gardens could be hiding-places, that words could be lies, that thoughts and intentions were not actions. From them I learned about contingency. Humankind invented contingency. I learned it from them. I had made them in my likeness, before grasping what I was. I gave them more than I knew I had, not knowing the power I was conferring on them. I gave them, in my naïve fondness for separation, what I could never have: I gave them each other. And with that, I had given them too much, allowing them powers of creation that I had not dreamed of. I did not know about imagination. I did not know about imagination doubled. I did not know about the idea of *us*. From the humans I made, I learned ————

———— They had different mothers, Abram and Sarai, so that might account for the difference in how they apprehended the world. But they had the same father, and that might account for the similarities between them. They

were enough alike and like their father not to have much
chance to slip through their allotted time without straining
at it. Or perhaps all that has nothing to do with it. He was a
man, and she was a woman. Similar, but different enough to
make a difference. Or were they just the way they were, each
of them, for no other reason than accident and variety?

One difference between them was that she knew there
weren't any certainties. Who can say why she knew such a
terrible thing? But she did, she seemed always to have
known that. He discovered a need for certainties so powerful that it nearly destroyed him. What it did to her is hard to
say. But it was his passionate wish for certainties that made so
much of the story his, and so little of it hers.

If certainty divided them, their love made each of them
inescapable for each other. Even when the difficulties began,
and even when everything changed, there was still love
between them, though it became a hard and bitter thing,
hidden, kept locked away by each in their own secret place.
Or was it the history of love, rather than love itself? Except
at the beginning, it was never an easy love, how could it have
been, sliding between the world's incompatible modalities
that were none of their making? None, I say, of any of our
making. But, interrupting and corrupting into innocence,
love began to do its sticky work.

Abram was ten years older than Sarai. A youth already by
the time she formed the first concrete picture of him that
would remain with her all her life. He was a marvel. A
prince of creatures. Though not then, in her first vivid
memory of him, to himself. And in retrospect, prince of
creatures hardly suited the swarthy, smouldering, sullen

young man four-year-old Sarai watched struggling with the material world. Deep shadows drew circles around the piercing black eyes, his cheeks and chin dark with a rush of adolescent stubble pushing frantically through the troubled, oily skin. His thick eyebrows, which met untidily and became one across the bridge of his nose, curved like a worry line, emphasising the sulky expression on the boy's face, as if it knew itself to have lost its heart-stopping childish beauty, but was not able to sense the transitory nature of its present coarseness. He was crabby with the heat of the day, his physical efforts and his own clumsiness.

They were in the storeroom of the workshop. Abram stood precariously on tiptoe on a pile of bricks, reaching up to a basket at the very top of the shelves above him. With his fingertips he was trying to knock the edge of the basket out of alignment to get a firmer grip on it, and cursing under his breath. Sarai lay on the floor watching the struggle. Below him Haran stood holding his arms up ready to receive the burden. The contrast between the two boys was startling. Haran, just a few years younger than his brother, still possessed the grace of pre-pubescent boyhood. His loose-jointed limbs fell effortlessly into elegant attitudes, as now, with his arms extended expectantly and his head thrown back, as if he were posing for an artist. His peachy skin was lit up by bright, eager, strangely blue eyes, and a mouth laughing in delight at the uncertainty of the present enterprise. Haran glowed with life, with life and his ignorance of its forthcoming complications, while his older brother grunted and sweated with the effort of making his unruly body perform as he wished. He struggled with his own awkwardness, wishing to reach higher, but being thwarted by his physical enemy. He wanted to perform the task as an adult, to confirm his authority, his dignity as the older, the stronger, the taller, but he felt himself humiliated in front of Haran and the baby, at least in his own eyes. Haran and Sarai were simply having fun, neither of them needing to display a dignity that was just out of reach. They enjoyed the game, while their brother was condemned, by his new-found inability to play, to do battle with intractable reality.

Sarai lay on the floor of the storeroom, slightly to one side of her big brother, and wriggled with pleasure at the adventure of retrieving the topmost basket. She laughed along with Haran at the marvellous uncertainty of the outcome as Abram reached, reached, but could not reach. His fingertips so near, but not close enough to get a grip on the edge of the basket and topple it into Haran's waiting arms. At any moment he might get there, his fingers inching minutely closer towards his goal, but never quite attaining it. Just another half-inch, quarter-inch, and then – Sarai could almost see it happening – the basket would suddenly lose its footing and pitch downward towards Haran, who would not be able to catch it properly, and collapse under its weight, so that he and it would land together in a heap on the floor, where she would join him in an anarchic scrummage until everything and all of them were fully coated with the powdered pigment that was its dusty contents. The present fun and the anticipated tumble had both Haran and Sarai squealing with laughter and excitement. But although she was laughing at the recalcitrant half-inch between her big brother's fingers and the substance of the basket, she was not, as he supposed, laughing at him.

However clumsy and oafish he might be feeling, to Sarai he was a resplendent being. Nothing that Abram did could diminish him in her eyes. While she rejoiced in the potential chaos of the situation, she was quite clear that it was the world she was having fun with. Abram, striving, even failing, against the world, remained her human champion. She could see the difference between Haran and Abram. She watched Haran glide through life, kicking and running after a stone as if his feet only touched the ground because he chose it. She could see how Abram was weighted to the earth, how awkward his movements were. How, reaching for the salt at meals, he would invariably knock over a pitcher of water; how rugs tripped him and tables struck him.

But of all the shadowy forms that she had grown to recognise in those earliest years, Abram grew to be the most admired, the most desired. Her mother and father became vital beings, necessary like air but too remote from her own condition to be models for her present infant world. Nahor, their oldest brother, was also an adult. Haran was other in a different way, a quicksilver presence, able, lovely to watch as he negotiated the world around him, but without authority, different, yet reminding her in some way of herself. Abram, however, stood between the child and the adults, an adult to Sarai's understanding, yet with something almost but not quite reachable about him that neither her parents nor Haran, let alone Nahor, could offer. He was simply complete. As she would be when she became whatever she was supposed to become.

Once the future had entered into her consciousness, in that earliest time, she understood that she was not to remain static in the infant world of her summer garden. That something was to be reached for. Some aim had emerged out of the aimlessness. The stillness in the garden was disturbed into a suspicion of altered destiny, of change, of a self different from the things around her, who stretched forward into more of herself, though what that more, or self, could be remained unknown until she understood Abram as a being that had become.

She became Abram's shadow, following him, watching him with close and anxious attention. She practised Abramness in her solitary hours, trying on his expression – worried concentration, sulkiness, an occasional sweet smile that emerged from the troubledness, just for his baby sister. She practised walking in his way, even bumping into the furniture and muttering the incomprehensible words he reserved for those collisions. She lowered her voice in an approximation of his gruff, monosyllabic way with words. She loved nothing better than to lie flat out on the workbench – when no adults were around – and watch him working on his figures, carving them as they had to be carved, gazing into his face, his eyes narrowed with concentration, with thought. She moulded mud in the hope that her efforts would coincide with Abram's figures, and practised concentrating by screwing up her face and sticking out her tongue, to indicate whatever monumental effort lay behind it.

Most of the time, Abram ignored his little stalker, used to having her under his feet or lurking beneath a table, and this too was part of his glorious maturity for Sarai. To be ignored by Abram was heaven. One day, she would achieve the status of ignoring some adoring shadow of her own. Every now and then he berated her when she got in his way – as if enough of the static world didn't already get in his way, he had to have a mobile obstacle to negotiate. He'd swat at her as if she were an annoying bug, or better still, chase her out of his presence, flapping his arms in exasperation. Sarai treasured such moments of attention. Then she would sneak back, silent as an ant, and he, grandly, had completely forgotten her, or pretended to. And sometimes, suddenly, he would shine himself at her. Turn his gaze towards her, call her name, pick her up and speak to her in a voice specially modulated for her alone. With Sarai on his lap, he would explain what he was doing: what the figure he made stood for, what it was meant to be. If the day was truly blessed, he would take her with him on an errand, out in the wide world, where everyone – even strangers passing through – could observe her with her hand enclosed in her big brother's hand, belonging to him, running to match his giant steps, being urged on: 'Come *on*, keep up.' *Me*, she would beam out to the passers-by, desperate for them to notice, *he's talking to me*.

Now, however, still huffing and puffing towards the basket, on top of his wobbling pile of bricks, Abram spoke in a different tone.

'Shut up, you two. This is serious.'

Clearly the struggle to reach the basket was not serious, but even Sarai understood that *something* was. Before the immediacy of this entertaining moment lay days in which the air had become fogged with anxiety. Something strange had come over their father. He had of late become more and more abstracted, thinking always about something else when he spoke. Sarai grew increasingly aggravated by his peculiar absence even while stroking her hair, or kissing her good-night. The other adults around her talked half the time in an undertone to each other, and sometimes to Nahor. There was a secret, but there wasn't the bubbling laughter under-neath their whispers that usually accompanied the kind of secrets that turned out to be treats and presents for the chil-dren. This was another kind of secret that Sarai had never come across before. And there was something about the whispering that made it a larger secret than the ones that usually concerned her. It was not just for her not to hear: it was as if the very walls of the house should be shut out of what the grown-ups were saying to each other. There was no question that seriousness was in the air, and that the basket-reaching entertainment was only a snatched inter-lude of relief for the uneasy younger children. Their gaiety at Abram's struggles was a welcome release from the secrecy and gloom that had gathered in their lives. And when, as expected, the basket finally tipped off the edge of the shelf, tumbling into Haran's arms to unbalance him, and Haran and Sarai finally rolled and squealed messily on the floor together amid its dusty contents, the hilarity went on rather longer than it should have, as if to keep the worried silence from returning. The beginning was already ending.

Their father, Terah, suffered from dark moods, which began to increase in intensity at around this time. Every few months, he started brooding and slowly pacing the courtyard, back and forth, back and forth, his great, bearish body bent forward with the effort of dragging his feet, his brow creased and dark, his head bowed, as if some doom-laden message were coming to him. Sometimes, he would shake his head as he walked, then stop and clutch it in his hands, as if trying to squeeze the thoughts out of it. The children learned to keep their distance when this happened. And then Terah would disappear for a time, and there would be much whispering and concern among the other adults of the household. Terah was nowhere to be seen or heard, though all of the rooms were open to the children, until some days later, when they would be playing in the corridors and hear weeping from a room they had just been told they were not to enter. No one explained these pacings and disappearances.

They say that at Terah's birth a plague of ravens had darkened the sky, swooping down on the corn seed even as it was being broadcast, and devouring it from the furrows before anyone had a chance to cover it with soil. A year of destitution followed. So it is said. It is also said (though never by her father) that Sarai's grandfather, the first Nahor, was a sooth-sayer and a magician, though he couldn't have been a very good one since he failed to predict the famine that would follow his son's birth, and a good deal else beside. Perhaps the augury foretold Terah's intermittently strange behaviour, or perhaps his moods came as a result of the fear of what it might have foretold. Perhaps those ravens one way or another had been responsible for everything and all of us. And perhaps they had been just a flock of passing birds. For all that, Terah was, between his bouts, as good and loving a father as any child might wish for.

The family could trace itself back ten generations, to an ancestor, Shem. Before that, nothing was known, though there was talk of a catastrophe that had destroyed the world; but how many families, in those days, or in yours, could count back so far? Later, she would learn more about this time before, but then, before Shem, all was mist. They were a respected clan, the Habiru, among the clans who had lived in Ur from time more or less immemorial.

During family prayers to Nanna, Sarai watched her father offering up libations to their household god as he ritually recited the names of his forefathers. When she was little, she would shut her eyes and listen to the rhythm of the names falling past her ears, one after another, soothing, hypnotic, like the sound of bright water dancing through a brook.

'These are the begettings of Shem: Shem begot Arpakhshad. And Arpakhshad begot Shelah. And Shelah begot Ever. And Ever begot Peleg. And Peleg begot Re'u. And Re'u begot Serug. And Serug begot Nahor. And Nahor begot Terah. And Terah begot Nahor, Abram and Haran.'

Though the sing-song of her father's voice kept its regular intonation and pace from start to finish, Sarai's excitement began to build like a spring winding up as he got half-way through, and then she would hold her breath with the tension of waiting as the list of unknown, unknowable beings crept towards the knowable present – Serug, whom she had only heard tell of; Nahor, her grandfather, still alive, though only just, when she was born; then Terah, her father, right there, in front of her, speaking those very words, reaching his own name; and then, the excitement peaked, Nahor, Abram and Haran, her beloved brothers, the present, them, all those generations reaching back into the blackness of nothing and arriving at their own living, breathing selves. Of course, there was always a pang at the final name that was never spoken. No mention of Sarai. Of the youngest, newest addition to the list. Of her. She knew, of course, that the women were not counted in the begettings, that she couldn't be there. But there was always a split second when she half hoped, waiting in the breathing space after 'Haran', for her father to pronounce the name *Sarai*. Naturally, he couldn't. He wouldn't even have thought of it. The ritual was fixed and solemn, one didn't play games with the moon god, it was not for mortals to change his rules. Or for a present generation to play with the tradition of the Habiru, handed down from father to son from all those generations ago. But often, in bed, in the hum of the night heat, she would say the begettings over to herself, like a story, or a poem, and then she would add a final 'Sarai', like a sigh, to the list of Terah's children. Since she wasn't actually making ritual obeisance to Nanna, she thought it would be all right. And surely, she thought, a great and powerful god like him wouldn't really mind a small child sticking her name at the end of a list. Anyway, he would be far too busy with important business even to notice.

'And Terah begot Nahor, Abram, Haran and *Sarai* . . .' ⸺⸺⸺

⸺⸺⸺ *I* made the beginning and I allowed the

begettings. The generation of generations was in my gift, as was everything. Reproduction was my invention, and with my permission – go forth and multiply – the humans replicated themselves. That more should come out of the unity was a novelty of my imagining. That the unity should be separated and a third come out of the two was, if I may say so, a masterstroke of elegance. Out of nothing I made companionship. I recognised the lack, though no such lack had ever existed before. I understood solitude, and I gave my creature company. Of he/she in my own image, complete of itself, of myself, I separated and divided and made two consciousnesses with the thought and the words to look at one another and say *I* and *you*. And what thanks did I get? How could I know that from the pair, the third is always excluded? No pair, no third existed before I made them. I found out.

I invented prohibition, they invented disobedience, so I invented punishment. Together, we were beginning to learn. I sent them away from the garden to live in the dust of the world. I gave them pain and difficulty – shame, they discovered for themselves and for me. From *us* to secrecy to shame. The sequence seems obvious now, but then it was all astonishment. I modelled my creatures from the dust and the rain, gave them life from my breath, gave them self-awareness with the Word, and then things undreamed of in the void followed. Consequences.

I condemned them to bring forth their generations in pain and hardship. I made it a very uncertain, life-threatening business. I liked the paradox – having gained a taste for paradox and other complications of the material world – of life threatening life. In any case, it kept things clear: reproduction was my process, freely given or not given at all. It also, of course, kept humanity in its place, the messy, dangerous business of conception and birth. I made them procreate that way to remind them that, like the beasts over which they had dominion, they were my beasts, of me, but not me. What need had I for reproduction, I am that I am? What use have I for a line, for verification of belonging, needing, loving and being loved? I am that I am.

And yet, once again, for all its absurdity and difficulty, these humans made more of reproduction than I had intended, took it for their own, blinded themselves to the real meaning behind it, and behaved quite as if it was their right to construct themselves a future and a history from the sticky insult of sexuality that I had condemned them to. They take and take, and then mistake all for their own. They made relation to one another – none to me. They made life of their own with the gift of reproduction that I have given all the living things I made. 'I have created a life,' she said, for all the world as if the lowest, squirming thing, crawling the face of the earth did not do the same. The human dared to think she could become like me. In my image I made them. And in my image they remade themselves ————

———— Sarai was all the more eager to add her name to the latest generation of the descendants of Shem, because she knew she wasn't entirely entitled to. Not just because she was a girl, but because she was not a full, proper sister to Nahor, Haran and her chosen Abram. Their mother,

Emtelai, was not her real mother. Sarai's mother had been a slave-girl whom Terah took into the household as his concubine when she became pregnant. She did not survive Sarai's birth, which was just as well because it was rumoured that Emtelai was not at all pleased with her husband's behaviour. She thought that what men do with slave-girls was their business, but when they bring them, big with child, into the home, it becomes household business, and Emtelai did not care much for sharing her house with another woman.

But Sarai was a different matter. Emtelai had provided the male heirs to the dynasty, but had failed to conceive again, being by the time of Haran's birth at the limit of child-bearing age. She was delighted at the prospect of having a baby girl after all the boys, and welcomed the baby, in her newborn motherless position, by adopting her as her own. Sarai did not even know the name of the woman who had given birth to her. Emtelai told her of her beginnings when she was old enough to understand, but assured her that she had become her mother in every way, except that Sarai had not shared Emtelai's womb like her brothers. Sarai called Emtelai mother, and believed herself to be completely accepted into the family. Even so, children think their thoughts. In her heart, she always knew that a line, as fine as the rarest silk, but a line nevertheless, existed between her brothers and herself.

Emtelai died when Sarai was eight years old. Perhaps Sarai was not quite enough for her, after all. Emtelai had become pregnant, in spite of her age. There was much celebrating among the family. Throughout her pregnancy, Terah did not once fall into one of his moods. Sarai thought she was happy, too. Emtelai said she hoped she would have a baby sister. She never made Sarai feel that she was about to be replaced by a more genuine article. But it was natural that the child, knowing herself not properly, not exactly and truly to belong to the family, should feel some anxiety at the coming arrival of someone new who did. It was natural that while she looked forward to having a little sister, to being no longer the baby of the family, just as Emtelai suggested, she might also find herself hoping that the new child would never appear. A small cloud gathered over Sarai's life during Emtelai's pregnancy. For the first time, a sense of foreboding, an uncertainty about the future that she didn't dare examine very carefully. It was no more than a tension in her chest, a nameless alarm, a dread or a wish that never worded itself into full awareness. In Sarai's heart, concealed deeply, the line between herself and the family thickened ever so slightly.

Emtelai died giving birth to Sarai's new sister, who was also born dead. It was not unusual: hadn't the woman who gave birth to Sarai died, leaving her to the family of Terah? But in this case, the child had died too, and no one was left except the already born. Nothing was added to the world, or to the family, except grief. Sarai missed Emtelai. Her mother's absence was palpable, as if death had created vacant places in the gaps where Emtelai should have been, in the air that should have carried her voice around the house. It was absurd, incomprehensible to Sarai that Emtelai was ir-retrievable, that nothing was left of her but memory, and that of the promised child not even that remained.

Terah performed all the necessary rituals, but it was as if

only part of him was there, and that in addition to the gaps where her mother should have been, there were gaps in the places where her father still was. And once Emtelai and the child were entombed in the space allotted to her in the family burial house, which should have been empty so much longer, he disappeared in actuality. It was a good many days before the children's own weeping was joined by the weeping in the room the children were forbidden to enter. Then Sarai and her brothers wept for their lost mother and their bereft father, too. They all wept that things had changed, and Sarai wept to see her brothers, especially Abram, weeping; for what solace could there be if they, if *he*, had none?

But Sarai wept also on account of her unaccountable wish, when Emtelai was alive, that the new baby would not come and change their lives. She recalled the shadowy cloud, that dread or wish she had felt at the news of her mother's pregnancy. The fear grew in her that the arrival of the cloud, the fact that she had somehow allowed it to exist and darken, even slightly, the joy at the news of the forthcoming child, made her in some way implicated in the deaths. With the death of Emtelai and the baby, the memory of her dark thoughts wrapped itself like a caul around her heart, and spun itself like a web to encase her mind: a new tightening, which she would learn eventually to live with, but which would never go away. A feeling as if something was scraping away at her insides came and never quite left. The taut shadows around her heart and her mind contained it, kept it within her, never to be brought to the light of day and never to escape. So, after all, something was added by her mother's death.

A life, a normal life, is whichever one you grow up living. And, then again, growing up, each thought, each unanticipated event leaves you wondering: Am I the only one in existence to whom such an idea, such a thing has occurred? It's not easy. Never was. Never will be. Some questions cannot be asked, not even of those you believe you can trust the most. What if the answer is *No, no one has ever thought such a thing before*? Worse, what if the answer, *That is perfectly normal*, is a lie given in kindness? You crave their love, but the love that others have for you makes them untrustworthy. And what of the result? Whatever the answer, how will they feel about you once you have asked the question?

How could eight-year-old Sarai tease out the words from the welter of emotions that came with the death of Emtelai and her child, and speak them to a beloved other? All she could remember was a rat gnawing away at the joy she felt that her adopted mother was going to have a baby. And then grief at their loss, mixed dreadfully with honeyed relief. Just the sensations, of course, not the words. How would she have expressed this? How could she have said the words even if she had found them? And to whom? To her devastated, despairing father, mourning his wife and child? To her idolised brother Abram, shocked pale at his loss of a mother? Even to formulate the words to herself would have emphasised her half-relation to those who were all she had in the world. Would they not have thought what she most feared they might think: that, no, she was not, after all, entirely one of them?

It was her earliest lesson in confusion and solitude, and in the limitations of love. She did not know whether half-thought thoughts, unwilled negative feelings, could cause the death of a woman and a child out in the real world. She feared perhaps they could. But she knew she could not ask anyone. She knew that the price for having had the bad thoughts, the terrible feelings, was that they must remain shut up inside her, unanswered questions that would make a question of everything she thought and felt for ever after. Anything was better than losing the trust of those who were everything to her. Any inner turmoil, even a lifetime of uncertainty, was better than tearing down the wall of love with which she was surrounded.

By the time Abram was eighteen, although he had never regained the lightness and grace of his young boyhood, he had come to better terms with the inevitability of manhood. Haran, although he had shot up in height and strength, nevertheless retained his luminous boyish quality. He was long-limbed and fair, unlike the rest of the family, with a curl at the sides of his mouth that was almost girlish. It was odd that he and Abram should have had the same parents. They seemed barely related. Abram had indeed grown through his clumsiness, but he was not tall, though strongly built, quite stocky, with short, muscular limbs. His face was broad all the way down, an expanse, where Haran's narrowed from the temples into a fine heart shape. Abram was solid, massive, even, like the stone and wood he chipped and carved into idols. He was much darker than Haran, with deep olive skin, Terah's heavy eyebrows, and Emtelai's thick black swathe of hair that fell to his shoulders, and sprouted, cropped close, around his mouth, cheeks and chin. His eyes were entirely his own, huge and slightly prominent, of an ebony so dark that they reflected the least shard of light around him, as if it flew into them by attraction to some inner illumination of their own. His strange and beautiful black eyes searched the world, wonderingly, until they came upon something that held them, and they fell with an intense stare upon whatever it was. Sarai still always hoped it would be her, and sometimes it was. He had grown older without growing away from her. She remained his little sister, and when he spoke to her, his voice would take on a warmth and amusement, just as it had done when they were both still children, back before their mother had died.

Sarai did not transfer her adoration to Haran just because he was more beautiful than Abram. How he looked did not matter. Abram was lodged in Sarai's heart as the meaning of the world, meaning in the world. Not, of course, that she didn't love Haran, or the more remote, entirely adult Nahor. Her spirits always leaped when she heard their footsteps entering the house, having finished their day at the workbench and the shop. She loved them like brothers, she loved her father like a father, but Abram she simply loved.

The brothers worked at the family business of making and selling idols to the citizens of Ur. They produced great carvings of Nanna, the creator god of the moon, and the other major gods of the twelve months and the seasons, for the temple, as well as making smaller idols for the household shrines of those and the less individual family gods that people would commission. Terah had retired and left the running of the business to Nahor, while he spent most of his time sitting in the courtyard, fanning himself slowly against the heat and the flies. Sarai, motherless, came and went as she pleased, from workshop to home and back again. She loved to watch her brothers working: making images out of formless chunks of wood or stone. But when she marvelled at Abram's skill in carving, he said she was too practically minded, that the form of the gods existed in the chunks all along, and that his skill was in seeing them right there, already waiting in the rough lumps of matter, so that his tools knew just where to chip and shave. She relished his certainty, but when she sat beside him at the bench with a piece of wood of her own, no matter how hard, or from what angle she looked, she could never see the form of the god in it. So she whittled.

'What's that?' Abram would ask as Sarai held up the sliver of sharp white wood that was all that remained after her whittling.

'That's the form that was in the piece of wood,' she would tell him, putting it on the bench, and picking up another piece to whittle.

'It's truly a wonder.' He would smile, with eyes mock-wide. 'You always find the wood with the long, thin, sharp god of all things long, thin and sharp. You must have a special affinity with him, Sarai. What is he called?'

'It's a *she*,' Sarai would tell him. 'And she has a secret name that no one can know. But she takes care of all the long, thin, sharp things in the world. And me.'

She painted and varnished each one with great care. There were several different colours. Families. A whole tribe of her goddess emerged, and she took each finished one home, to join the rest. When she wearied of the workshop, she would marshal her tribe and have them lead their lives.

Caravans of red ones would arrive from the desert carrying all manner of strange and wonderful goods from far away, and the yellow town dwellers would buy them in the market, give them to their children if they were good, take them away if they were bad. There were wars and alliances, too. But the first stick she whittled remained the great goddess, who oversaw the well-being of her tribe, and lay apart thinking god-like thoughts. She was called Sarai, though Sarai never told this to her father or brothers when they came across her playing and asked about the one lying alone.

They lived well, a respected family in the community. The priest admired their work, even the mighty Hammurabi would order his idols from their workshop. Life was orderly, urban and as comfortable as any in the world. It is true that they were surrounded by desert, and that for food they, like everyone in Ur, were dependent on the nomadic herdsmen and the caravans bringing grain; but Hammurabi was wise, and built granaries which stored surplus grain against the times of famine. Aside from the loss of her mother, and the tightness around her heart, which she only noticed from time to time – as the light faded, in the blackness of the night before she slept, sometimes when she was playing with her whittled tribe and became aware of the isolation of the goddess Sarai in a special way – her life was good. All their lives were good.

So at first, when Haran started to behave oddly, it seemed to be just the ordinary wildness of a young man. He disappeared for days and returned with dark rings under his limpid eyes and a sullen look around his beautiful mouth. Sarai overheard her other brothers worrying about him. He absented himself from the workshop and was drinking much more than he should. He was also pursuing women, bad ones, according to her brothers. But he would grow out of it, they said to each other, while lecturing him about decent behaviour and family reputation.

One day, two or three years after the death of Emtelai, Nahor returned home with an infant in his arms. The boy was just a few days old and a wet nurse was found for him. Sarai, of course, was delighted.

'His name is Lot. He's your nephew,' Nahor told her, as he put the swaddled baby in her arms for the first time.

She loved him instantly, feeling his warm, damp breath against her cheek as she kissed his tiny face and the strength of his minute fist clamping itself around her finger if it got anywhere within his reach. She ignored her tribe of whittled wood and devoted herself to adoring Lot and being his aunt. She was aware that, like her, Lot was not entirely of the family. Although Terah adopted him she understood that Haran was his father. No mention was ever made of his mother, as no mention was made of Sarai's. She felt the baby and she had something in common. Terah, though reticent at first, could not resist Lot's babyish gurgles and smiles, and soon had him on his lap, or lying beside him in his shaded crib in the courtyard. Haran took no interest in the child on his rare appearances in the family home. Nahor was kindly but distant, while Abram looked with wonder on the child as if his every movement and expression were some code he had to unravel. And he, like Sarai, loved the warm livingness of the tiny creature in his arms. Though Lot was a great addition to her life, Sarai was disturbed by the change in

Haran. It seemed to threaten the calm and regularity the family had found for themselves after the death of Emtelai.

Sometimes, when the older people were together, sipping sweet tea, Sarai would hear them grumbling about how civilisation was crumbling. How good and orderly things had been in their youth, how a person could walk the streets of the city without fear of encountering young people intent on foolishness or harm. They worried that all that had been gained from the wilderness of the past was about to be lost. That life would revert to its original primitive state of chaos because something was wrong with the young. They no longer feared their parents, they no longer feared their gods. They had nothing but material pleasure on their minds, and gave no thought to practical consequences or the retribution of the gods. Nahor, who was married now to Milcah, and seemed to Sarai to belong to that generation, joined in with this talk. But when Sarai asked Abram about it, he shrugged.

'Old people fear the young. They always have and always will,' he said, concentrating on his carving. 'I should think Father's father spoke with his friends like this about Father and his friends. In three thousand years from now, the old will still be worrying about the world going crazy and civil-isation coming to an end.'

Even then there was something of the prophet about him.

But there were streets in the city where it was inadvisable for a person on their own to walk in the dark. And Sarai knew that Abram, Terah and Nahor were all worried about Haran's wildness.

'What is the matter with Haran?' Sarai asked.

Abram frowned and stopped carving.

'I don't think it's to do with the times we live in. There's something inside Haran that rages against . . . I don't know what, not exactly. The way things are, have been, why . . . Perhaps he doesn't know, and that's why he gives himself up to dissolute ways.'

Sarai loved it when Abram forgot she was a child and spoke his thoughts to her. She did not ask him what dissolute ways were in case it reminded him of her youth.

'Doesn't Haran love us any more?' she wondered. 'Doesn't he fear the gods? That's what Father says. I overheard him say that Haran went into the workshop one night and broke the idols. Just whacked off their heads with a stick.'

'He was drunk,' Abram explained, but he looked very troubled. 'I think he wants to fear the gods. But there is something in him that rebels against all authority. And he fears, too, that he doesn't fear the gods. So he challenges them, like he challenges his family with drunkenness and . . .'

'Lot,' she suggested.

'Yes, and Lot.'

'What will the gods do? Won't they be very angry at being smashed?'

'He broke models, Sarai. The things we made are just images of what we worship. They aren't the actual gods themselves. If we could make gods in this workshop we'd be more than the gods, wouldn't we? We'd be creating them. No, Haran just broke pieces of wood and the gods will understand. Our family gods will protect him. He'll calm down and come back to us.'

But he didn't. He didn't get the chance. One morning

before dawn, Sarai woke to the sound of terrible wailing, even more desperate than the cries she heard at Emtelai's death. She ran to Terah's room and found him tearing at the air, surrounded by the servants and her brothers, Nahor and Abram, trying to calm him, but looking distraught themselves. Sarai stood in the doorway, and saw in Terah's eyes a wild hopelessness she had never seen before. He howled like an animal, wrenching away from the arms of his sons trying to catch and contain him. Abram saw her and took her in his arms.

'Is Father ill? Is he dying?' she asked in a terrified whisper.

Abram's eyes were overflowing with tears.

'A terrible thing has happened,' he said, holding her tightly, so that he was whispering gently in her ear. 'An accident. Haran. Very bad.' There was a sob and he stopped speaking.

'Has Haran been hurt?'

'He's gone. We've lost him.'

'Gone where? Won't he come back?'

'Haran has died, Sarai.'

She couldn't take it in. Old people died. Women in childbirth died. Babies died. But beautiful young men, frantic with energy, glowing with life, didn't die. Her laughing, blue-eyed brother reaching up to catch a falling basket couldn't have died. And aged fathers, who might once have wept for dead wives and infants, did not weep for the death of a youthful son. The sons wept for the fathers. It was the way of the world. Sarai knew that. How could such a travesty have happened? Had such a thing ever happened before?

'Was he ill? I saw him yesterday and he wasn't ill.'

Abram didn't answer. He picked her up and carried her back to her bed. She fell asleep eventually with him stroking her hair with one hand, while the other covered his eyes in an effort to contain his tears.

The grieving in the house of Shem was very great. Yet they did not go to the temple to share their sorrow with the gods and the people of the city. They did not even pour funeral libations at the family shrine. This grief was huddled and horrified. No outsiders came to console Terah as they had when Emtelai had died. A curious silence settled over the house, as if the wall around the courtyard not only contained the weeping that occurred within but kept the whispers of the world outside. Haran was buried in the dead of night, unceremoniously, and only Sarai's father and brothers were present when they placed him in the tomb alongside his mother and baby sister.

After the burial no one spoke of him again. The silence was omnipresent. Whatever they were speaking of, they were always not speaking of Haran. Sarai couldn't understand why. In her life she had known a sense of strangeness: with her own semi-alienation and her father's moods, she had experienced love and loss in the everyday life of the family, but this was her first encounter with blank mystery. Her father's grief was more than mourning the loss of his son. He refused to set foot outside the house. Soon, Abram and Nahor were at home all day. No one mentioned the work-shop. Nahor and his wife increasingly kept to themselves, and Nahor spent many hours at the family shrine, muttering and making sacrifices. Only the baby, Lot, behaved nor-

mally, laughing and gurgling, struggling to crawl, grasping at
ankles. Sarai spent a great deal of time with him. Even
Abram was distant. He seemed to keep her at an arm's
length. She supposed he feared her childish questions.

This went on for many weeks. The house became dark
and silent. Nahor and Milcah kept to their own quarters and
were the only ones to leave the house. No one came to
them, except one or two remote relatives from the city, who
came at night and sat in a baffled silence as Terah rocked
back and forth with his head dropped in his hands.
Sometimes he murmured, 'What reason? Why?' But no one
tried to answer his question.

Some weeks after Haran's death Sarai learned what had
happened from a sweetly persistent friend of her own age
who visited her against his parents' orders.

'They said I mustn't come here. Your family is defiled.'

Neither of the children knew what that meant, but they
both agreed that it sounded awful.

'They said you would be punished, all of you. That your
brother des–desecrated the temple.'

'But he died. He was ill, he must have been, because he
was so young and he died.'

'No, he wasn't ill.'

'How could he have died if he wasn't ill?'

'He did it himself. Made himself die. He cut himself and
all the blood in his body poured out. He cut his throat open
at the foot of Nanna's shrine, and the blood spurted all over
Nanna. And when the priest found him in the morning,
Nanna's face had been chipped away, so it was just a blank.
Haran did it before he cut himself. That's why no one will

buy idols from your brothers, and they closed the workshop. You're all forbidden to enter the temple. The house of
Shem is unclean.'

There was no animus in her friend's voice. He compre-
hended it as little as Sarai did, and was just reporting what
he'd heard from the adults. But she shoved him hard enough
to make him fall over when he finished speaking, and then
ran back into the house shouting, 'We don't want to go to
the temple, anyway.'

The family disgrace did not disturb her thoughts as much
as the image of her lovely Haran's blood spilling from his
body, or the unbearable idea that he had deliberately drawn
a knife across his throat. Worst of all, most strange, was his
wish to die. Sarai could not imagine what such a feeling
must be like, or what terrible suffering would have been
contained in such a mad desire. She tried to feel his pain as
the most awful she had known, but nothing she had ever felt
had made her want to let the lifeblood out of her body. Her
mind squirmed at the horror he must have suffered before he
did such a terrible thing.

Sarai ran to Abram and sobbed on his chest.

'I don't know. I don't know,' he murmured miserably at
her wailings. 'He spoke to me once of doubt. Doubt about
everything. It was as if he woke up one day and didn't
believe in the world any more. Perhaps it had something to
do with Father's moods. I don't know. Something in Haran
would not leave him alone. Wouldn't let him live.'

He wasn't speaking to Sarai any more, although he still
rocked her in his arms. He was trying to explain to himself
what had not been talked of for weeks. He didn't sound

convinced, but it was a relief to Sarai just to hear the sound of Haran's name being spoken for the first time since he left them. It may have been a relief to Abram to speak it ————

————   I might have brought the whole experiment to an end, there and then, with that first human birth, but I had discovered anger, and with what could I be angry if I destroyed the object of my anger? And I was curious, too. So much had come from so little. So much consequence. What else might these helpless individuals have to show me?

Death, of course. I knew nothing of death as they invented it. How could I? I had created life. I had to ask the boy, the farmer, where the shepherd was, just like I had to ask the first pair where they were in the garden that I had made for them. Hiding, always hiding. From the boy, a shrug. The first shrug. 'Am I my brother's keeper?' All new to me. Brother? And that denial of something I had never even envisaged: responsibility to one another. They had made relationship and obligation, and with their perversity immediately negated what had never been thought before. Am I my brother's keeper? I just wanted to know where the lad was. The scent of roasted sheep meat pleased me. It was a new sensation in the world I had made. And it had stopped. It was an innocent enough question. But suddenly, there was a family. And suddenly, there was death.

By any logic, if death was going to occur on the earth, it should be of my will. Yet now they went beyond me.

Appropriating creation and devising its end also. No death had happened until then. I had not invented it when I made the first he/she. To tell the truth, it hadn't occurred to me. Yes, I warned them in the garden that I would destroy them if they disobeyed my single prohibition, but that was my prerogative. Dust to dust. Destruction. And when they disobeyed me anyway, did I destroy them? No, I did not. I made life difficult, but I did not – check it and see – destroy them. Indeed, I told the woman that she would become the mother of all the living, and I made them coats of skin, when I sent them into the wilderness, and with my own hand clothed the nakedness they were making such a fuss about. I was angry, but I promised and comforted as well as punished. I did not kill them.

It crossed my mind, though, that I had not taken life-span into account. Were my creatures to live for ever? Clearly not: only eternity and the I am that was once within it could do that. I had, however, made no particular arrangements about the end of the life I had created. I needn't have worried. Cain, the sedentary farmer, first born of the first born, took care of that.

'What have you done?' I cried at the boy, as the scent of Abel's roast lamb was replaced by something new and altogether more acrid rising from the earth. Eve discovered she could make life, like me. And her son found he could destroy it, before any such thing was on my mind. Cain had taken life, my life, the life that I had made. Did I kill him? No, I condemned him to wander the face of the earth for his impertinence. 'But without protection, anyone could kill me,' he whined. The cheek of it. No one was killing anyone before he started it. Now, he wanted protection. I should have smitten him there and then. But how would that have countered this further appropriation of my power? I resolved to outlaw death caused by any other hand but mine. I made a new rule, and gave Cain a mark, so that all should know that death was my business. Of course, the rule was already breached before I made it, but what else could I do? It seemed I was always to be one step behind these humans ————————

———————— Eventually, the isolation and the shame became too much. In any case, the family could no longer make a living in Ur. One morning Terah called his sons, the servants, Lot's nurse and Sarai into the courtyard. He sat in his chair as usual, his face fallen, his eyes reddened as they had been ever since his younger son had died.

'We must prepare to leave this place,' he announced, in a voice that was more a groan than a declaration. 'We will find another city and begin again to build a name for our family. We will redeem the wrong done by . . .' He could not name the name, nor even his relation to him. It was pitiful. He looked so old, far too old and weary to be talking of starting again. He looked like one for whom everything had been over for too long. He drew a breath. 'I have two strong, skilled sons, a good daughter, and . . . and a grandchild. We will leave this place. We will make a new life.'

Nahor stepped forward. 'Not me,' he said. 'I will not give up everything because of what that foolish boy did to us.'

There was an astonished silence. Terah had not been asking, he had come to a decision and was telling the family what the future would be.

'Are you not of our family?' he asked, too quietly.

'Perhaps I am not,' Nahor replied, just as quietly. 'And perhaps if I was not, I could live here with Milcah and make a family of my own. One I need not be ashamed of. It will be better if you go and live somewhere else. I will remain here.'

Terah looked at him for a long moment. Then Nahor took Milcah by the arm and left the gathering.

'Two sons dead,' Terah whispered, while Sarai looked towards her beloved Abram, her last brother, standing stock still with grief, and realised that they both stood in the ruins of their world.

So normality ends, cataclysmically. Perhaps the seeds of the cataclysm are sown in the normality itself; perhaps the cataclysm is merely a part of the normality. How would a young girl know? How would anyone know? Then or now. Nothing more than bad fortune, perhaps: a flock of ravens passing over a clear blue sky. But accident is too terrible a thought for a child in the midst of a cataclysm. To Sarai, as she pondered it in the wreckage of the wall of love that had surrounded her all her years, there seemed to be a pattern, a movement, and it was one in which she seemed to be most dreadfully implicated. It began when Emtelai and the baby died – or worse, when Emtelai told Sarai of the impending birth and the small cloud arrived and hovered over them. Then Terah's mood darkened permanently, and Haran killed himself, and Nahor left the family, and now they were to tear up their roots and head off into the desert. All these things occurred, as they had not occurred to any other family Sarai had known, and they seemed to her, these things, to follow one another, and finally, to follow one from another. They were to leave the wall of love behind them, a ruin, and Sarai was to live with the secret knowledge that it was she who had wrenched away the first stone.

And yet this terrible burden she was to carry was itself nothing more than ordinary. As ordinary as beginning in the garden and discovering desire, as ordinary as the longing to become the object of one's infantile desire. The omnipotent and fearful belief that you alone have caused a crack in normality. That your growing private thoughts have torn apart a world that would have survived intact for eternity had you never been born into it. Fear, sadness, confusion, doubt and loss: the consequences of separateness and the creation of love. Just part of being born and participating in the human dance. No one escapes.

Leaving

And Abram and Nahor took them wives: the name of Abram's wife
was Sarai; and the name of Nahor's wife, Milcah . . . But Sarai was
barren; she had no child. And Terah took Abram his son, and Lot
the son of Haran his son's son, and Sarai his daughter in law, his
son Abram's wife; and they went forth with them from Ur of the
Chaldees, to go into the land of Canaan . . .
GENESIS 11:29–31

The disgraced remnant of the family of Shem set off into
the desert. They had an initial destination: Harran. Travellers
had told Terah of this city, in which, though far away to the
north-west of Ur, the inhabitants worshipped the same
familiar gods. Perhaps the family skills could be used there,
where their disgrace was not known. They were headed for
a place where it seemed possible that they might remake
their old life: like and unlike. The name probably counted
for something, though it was pronounced more gutturally
than the name of Sarai's dead brother. Perhaps it gave Terah
some pleasure to name the place when he could no longer
name the son.

It was a small party, just the close family (minus Nahor
and Milcah), Lot and his nurse, Nikkal, and those few servants who were willing to go with them. They left in the
dead of night, like criminals, like the outcasts that they now

were, their movable possessions packed on a line of asses. The plan was to trade goods and pick up some livestock on the way, so that they might have a source of food and seem much like other desert wanderers. There were six hundred miles of wilderness to cover before they could return to any kind of normal life. But what did they know about the care of sheep and goats? They had had servants to buy the animals in the market, servants to cook them: they had eaten their flesh, sacrificed lambs and kids to the gods, but rear them, travel with them? Terah resisted the idea of giving up their urban identity to become 'carers of beasts, of stinking, stupid animals'. But Abram insisted. He would learn to care for them, he assured his father, and the journey would be safer if they appeared to be like the other nomads they would come across, rather than a wealthy citified family with all their worldly goods, helpless in the desert.

'We *will* be helpless in the desert,' Terah replied, from within his cloud of gloom.

'We will learn not to be,' Abram said, his fierce black eyes already turned away from Ur to a new life.

This, of course, made Terah feel much worse.

'That I should have to learn a new life, and such a life, at my age . . .' and he sank his head in his hands and began to sob.

But Sarai was young enough to be quite excited about an entirely new way of life. She had often watched the nomadic children when they came to the city, wild and free creatures, they seemed, strong and sunburned, and with a grasp of the world and their place in it that she envied. She wondered if she could be like them, once they had left the loving yet constraining wall of her house for the open spaces of the desert.

Sarai was thirteen by the time they set off for Harran. During that first week of desert living, walking and riding by dawn and dusk in the sand-blown emptiness, sleeping in the heat of the day and under layers of rugs in the iciness of the night, she had her first period. She went to Abram, afraid that her life was pouring away.

'I'm ill,' she told him. 'Blood is leaking from my body.'

Abram lowered his eyes. 'You must talk to Nikkal,' he said, without looking at the girl. 'She will explain.'

Sarai was surprised by Abram's lack of surprise, and by his refusal to explain what clearly he understood. He had never before evaded her questions if he had any kind of an answer. She stared at him, fearing the unimaginable worst.

'It's women's business,' he said, with finality.

Nikkal told the astonished Sarai about the process of reproduction. She was not surprised at the girl's shock, which now replaced the fear Sarai had had that she might have a life-threatening illness.

'Every month? I'll bleed every month?'

'You're a woman now. It shows that you can bear children of your own.'

Sarai had never doubted that she could. That was what all women did. But that it required a monthly blood-letting was strange and terrible. Blood was sacred. It was spilled only to honour or placate the gods. Then it was called sacrifice, and the creature sacrificed forfeited its life. What was more precious than blood, which was life itself? New life, apparently. And yet how could she forget what she had heard from her friend in Ur? The image of Haran's blood spurting from his throat, emptying him of life, flashed hideously into her mind. His death; Sarai's assurance of new life. That Nikkal should be so calm at her flow of blood when Haran's had caused such grief and turmoil was a mystery she could not fathom. How could she not feel terror at the sight of the bright fresh blood dripping down her thighs, and the thick, dark clots that issued from the very centre of herself?

That night she wept for more than just her horror of spilt blood. She was unclean, Nikkal had told her. She must not approach her father or brother while her period was flowing. She must keep to herself, to the company of women, and then, when the bleeding was over, she had ritually to wash and pour a libation to the gods. Every month. She was no longer free to hang about her beloved Abram, or stroke her father's knee whenever she wanted. She was no longer a child. She was a mother in waiting. A creature quite different from men. Dangerous, even. Necessary but contaminating. Closer, in her ritual uncleanliness, to her poor, disgraced brother Haran than to the rest of her family.

'Why?' she asked Nikkal.

'I've heard stories,' she said.

She told Sarai an ancient tale of the beginning of the world, quite unlike their own story of the beginning. It was something women knew, because women had always asked, as she had, why the birth of children should mean such trouble for them alone. It was whispered between them during the time of their uncleanliness.

'It's just a story,' Nikkal said.

But it was the strangest story Sarai had ever heard, about

a single god, alone in the universe, who made and punished and destroyed at will, and a humanity entirely at his mercy. Of course, the gods of Ur destroyed too. There had been a flood long ago in their history, but only one god among many was responsible, and other gods tempered his fury and the effects on humanity. The Babylonians had their champions in the pantheon. These other stories that the women told each other, and it was now Sarai's turn to hear, left her with a sense of helplessness, a sense of being without anyone on her side. It was terrible, but apt as the first blood leaked from her own body and she learned that this was a reality over which she was to have no control.

'Don't speak of this to men,' Nikkal warned her. 'The priests would accuse us of blasphemy. It's women's business.'

'Don't the men know about it?'

'There must be some things men don't know about. They don't know about bleeding and childbearing. Rather, they don't think about what it means for women, they care only for the results. Let's keep it to ourselves and have some stories of our own.'

'But it's such a terrible story. Can't we pour libations to this god? Can't we do anything to change his mind?'

'You have too much faith in the gods' concern for us. Anyway, I didn't say the other story was true. We tell it to each other to explain why we have so little choice in our lives as women. Men's stories don't concern themselves with that.'

'So it isn't a true story?'

'Does it describe your situation as you have just discovered it to be?'

'It seems to.'

'Then it's true enough. That's as true as human stories can get.'

Sarai imagined the long stretch of life ahead of her, and the uncountable months of bleeding and isolation.

'Every month, until I die?'

Nikkal smiled.

'No, eventually the monthly flow will dry up. And then you will be relieved, but also, believe it or not, grief-stricken. Then you will conceive no more babies and you will grow old. The thing has started and, from now on, the course of your life will be marked by blood and its absence. Everything will stem from its appearance and disappearance. It is the way of the world. You are one of the women, now. One of us.'

She made it sound a dubious privilege.

That night, as Sarai wept at her new alienation from Abram – how many days would it be before she could fling her arms around his neck and see him smile at her childish adoration? – she heard his voice coming from Terah's tent. They were talking in urgent tones, her father insistent, Abram arguing, but their voices were lowered so it was not possible to make out what they were saying. It was not until her period was finished and she had been ritually cleansed that she discovered what they had been talking about.

She was called to Terah's tent as soon as her ablutions were over. She ran to him with relief, and hugged him, climbing into his lap as she had always done. He kissed her gently on the cheek, but eased her off his knees, telling her to sit on the stool in front of him. He was not unkind, only intent on creating a new distance between them. Sarai was mortified, but as she sat, he reached out and took her hand, holding it cupped between his palms.

'They say you are a woman now,' he said, with a sad smile and a slow shake of the head.

Sarai couldn't say anything, the thought of the blood flowing between her legs, and of her father knowing about it, perhaps everyone knowing about it, was too shaming.

'It's a sign, that it should have happened now. A sign that the family of Shem will not be destroyed by the troubles that have fallen on us. From you will come new life, we will grow through you, and our losses, my lost sons and their offspring, will be made good.'

Sarai listened without understanding.

'Your children will make us strong again. A new generation. You must be married.'

Still, she listened; still, she failed to understand. Whom could she marry in this desert? Whose children could she have that would enlarge the family of Shem? Was she to be given to some passing group of nomads? How would that help their clan? If this was to happen now, who was there? Surely, Lot, her nephew, was the hope of the family's continuation, and he was still just a baby. How could she bear children who would remain within their bloodline?

'If Lot were older,' Terah said, seeming to read her thoughts. 'But we cannot wait for so long. We need the strength of a new generation now, as we head for a new life. Sarai, these are desperate times. You are different from my other children, apart from them, born from another womb.'

She felt a stabbing pain around her heart at these words. It had never been said in such a way before.

'But Emtelai said she adopted me, that she had become my mother.'

'Yes, yes, of course. But now it turns out to be for the good, as if it had been meant. You are one of us, but also distant enough. You can be married to Abram, and your children will truly be a new generation of our family.'

'Married to my brother?'

'He is your half-brother. It will do,' Terah said, nodding resolutely into the distance as if to elicit the agreement of someone who stood behind Sarai. But there were only the two of them in the tent.

'Abram's wife?' She said the words only to hear them spoken aloud.

'The new mother of our people. You will be the matriarch that the generations to come will all look back to.'

'Abram's wife?' she breathed again.

'Sarai,' Terah said gently, 'it is unusual, but it is not impossible. It is necessary. You're fond of Abram. He has always been your favourite. He is a good man, sturdy, solid, responsible. He understands the importance of family. Who would look after you better than him? Whom could you trust more than him? It's not perfect, perhaps, but these are not perfect times. We have no other choices. We must not die out, we must not dilute the family. Ideally, we would wait for a child of Lot and yours . . . but we must do what we must. Can you understand? You are a clever child, surely you can understand the importance of keeping the family going?'

Sarai just managed to stop herself from whispering, 'Abram's wife,' for a third time. But she could hardly concentrate on what Terah was saying for the way the phrase bounced around in her head all the while. She was to become her beloved brother's wife. Her beloved *half*-brother's wife, as her father had corrected her for the first time in her life.

She left Terah's tent having had her deepest longing and most dread fear realised simultaneously – and discovered the longing and the fear to be so inextricable as to have been virtually identical all along. As a small child she had cuddled up to Abram and whispered to him that she was going to marry him when she grew up, that she would never leave him and that they would be together always. Abram laughed and said she would feel differently when she was older, and would want to make a life with someone else. Terah would find a suitable young man whom she would come to love and cherish. Someone with melting eyes and soft cheeks who would sweep her off her feet. Someone outside the immediate family, so that new ties were made and the family enlarged. It was the way of the world.

'Someone I don't know?' she would shudder.

'Someone you don't know yet.'

She would shake her head vigorously. She would only ever want Abram. She was going to stay with him for ever.

'Please don't marry anyone before I'm old enough to marry you,' she would beg him. 'Wait for me.'

Apart from her childish love for Abram, she had wanted also to be enclosed for ever within the family that she secretly feared she was not entirely part of. It was as if she could only truly be a full member if she remained a beloved child of the house, if she were contained for ever within the wall of love that protected her from not quite belonging. All the while she was a child, no one had called her *half*-sister. And yet, it turned out now that only by being called half-sister was her immature dream of being for ever Abram's loved one going to come true. And so the way of the world was subverted into her deepest desire precisely by what she dreaded most. As her father had said *as if it had been meant*, all her hopes and fears exploded into reality. Her dreams came true and, of course, translated from wish to life, were quite different from anything she had imagined.

But (she had so much to learn, she still knew so little. Oh, my heart) as soon as they were betrothed, Abram began to keep a terrible distance from Sarai. Even when he came directly upon her, he would avert his eyes, look down at the dust and sand, off to one side, anywhere rather than let his gaze rest on her. He would mumble something that seemed to contain no words and even less affection and pass hurriedly on, always with some urgent business to attend to. He never spoke to her after her interview with Terah; it was as if their forthcoming marriage had severed the lifetime of love and comfort they had between them. And yet sometimes she would turn on an impulse and catch him looking at her from a safe distance with the strangest expression she had ever seen in the face she thought she knew so well. He would immediately turn away, but not before Sarai had observed him. No one had ever looked at her that way before: the familiar affection turned to something darker, more intense, his eyes burning towards her as if he were seeing something – *her*, for heaven's sake – for the first time. It frightened her a little, but although she suffered anguish at the sudden loss of easy contact with him, she thought a lot about this new Abram she fleetingly glimpsed, and brought his face with that new look to her mind's eye, savouring it. Why, she really did not know. It was her last moment of true innocence ――――――

―――――― Ten human generations on and humankind had taken my exhortation to be fruitful and multiply to their hearts. Rather, to their loins. These creatures, which I had made analogous to myself, took image for reality. Mistook their image for my reality and believed themselves real, simply because their flesh – the roughest of metaphors for eternal existence – took up space in the world. With their flesh they recreated and re-created, with their flesh they destroyed and were destroyed: and so they believed that the flesh itself was proof of life, instead of a poor necessity resulting from the nature of the nature I happened to make.

First disobedience, then death, and now the pleasures of the flesh became the next fine invention of my creatures. And I am no fool: in each of these moves, they were asserting their authority – reaching beyond their remit as my creatures, licensed on earth, in my likeness, made to reflect my likeness to myself – to imagine themselves sufficient unto themselves.

The few had turned into the many. A great proliferation occurred over those ten generations, a mass of them, which they took to be greater than my singularity, and all conversation stopped between them and me. I was alone again. In all that time, after Cain, I took no interest, let them get on with imagining that they were lords of their own universe. I did not care. I would not care. I retreated into silence. I turned my face from their insouciance towards eternity. I let life and death and all its murky consequences swamp the earth I had so meticulously ordered.

But from the ordure, a single quavering voice finally reached my awareness, calling out to me against the tidal wave of concupiscence. I turned to look at the earth again, and heard the pleading of a single man, Enoch, and saw what a mess humankind had made of my world. I did that man a favour, and took him out of the ugliness only he seemed to have the misfortune to recognise, and mingled him into eternity, thinking he was the last who would walk in my way, and that rescuing him was the last I would ever have to do with humanity. Yet once I had looked on my formerly sweet and empty earth, I found it hard to look away. And an anger rose in me, unlike anything I had experienced before.

They had got on with their lives, these humans. They were resourceful with my resources. They had built cities, and used the substance of the earth itself to fashion their wants. Forged metal into tools, carved rock and woven vegetation into shelter, ornament and musical instrument. What did they need me for? And in the dead of night, when neither cities, nor tools, nor walls, nor music quite soothed their fear at the smallness and vulnerability of the human condition, they turned and grasped each other in a bid for solace. The world I made was a ruin, a seething mass of flesh hacking away here and constructing there in a fervour of activity, all held together with the mutual self-comfort of gluey sexual desire. There they were, discovering this, that and each other. And of me, there was not a thought ————————

———————— Their father married Abram and Sarai in his tent in a ceremony that barely deserved the name. In front of the statues of Nanna and the other household gods, Terah intoned the begettings, leaving out the names of Haran and Nahor while adding Lot to the end of the list, as was usual these days. Sarai's name was still absent, but on that occasion everyone noticed it, not her alone. They hardly constituted a congregation, their tiny tribe and servants, but they managed a marriage feast, sharing the youngest, most succulent lamb of their small flock with the gods. It was a quiet affair, perhaps the first quiet wedding in history.

Sarai's personal things had been moved from the tent she shared with Lot and Nikkal into Abram's. After the feast, he escorted her to her new quarters and dropped the flap behind them. A separate sleeping place had been made up for Sarai. She turned to Abram. 'Nikkal has told me about being a married woman.'

It was almost a question. What Nikkal had told her, about the matter of getting babies and wifely duties, she vaguely knew already from other children. She gave Sarai no more than the general details, adding that it was the lot of a woman to do whatever her husband wished. But nothing she and her friends had talked about, or Nikkal spoke of, had anything to do with *Abram*. Husbands, duty, lying under the heavy weight of a man, receiving his seed, all that she could take in, but Abram was Abram. Even at that moment in the tent, she could only feel that she was with her darling ever-helpful Abram, not alone for the first time with her new husband. She appealed to him for guidance as to what to feel or think or want or do. She expected her brother to comfort her in her confusion, to sort out and ease the difficult situation she now found herself in. Instead, he turned his back, threw a cloak over his fine wedding clothes, and for the first time in days spoke to her in a clear, deliberate tone. 'One of the ewes is due to lamb. I must go and check on her.'

And he left her.

This was the real beginning of Sarai's life as a woman. It took her very much longer to understand, but what she learned then was how little Nikkal had told her about what being a woman meant. The sexual explanation was nothing, mere mechanics, compared to this new relation she discovered she had to the world, and the sudden loss of childhood expectation that others would know more, and help her through the mysteries and difficulties. She had felt alone with her confusion ever since the death of Emtelai and the baby, but it was bewilderment and aloneness of her own making. This new distress was not a secret of her heart, it was a sense of being lost in the real world and of not knowing how she was supposed to live in it. It was not a private terror, it concerned others. It concerned, above all, her trusted brother Abram. Yet she was abandoned on this most confusing night of all by the one person to whom she would instinctively have turned for help. He would not help, and she was left alone to try to understand what was impossible for her to grasp: that he *could* not help, that his confusion was as great as hers. He had no better idea of how a brother and sister might become husband and wife than Sarai, and it was worse for him, perhaps, because he was older and understood how deep the confusion was. She only knew there was a new stranger in her life, and that he had been the person she trusted most in all the world.

Sarai took off her pretty clothes and slipped under the rugs of her bed. It had been placed at the back of the tent, behind Abram's mattress. She blew out the lamp and lay in the dark, listening. There were no sounds from the other tents, just the wind whistling in the cold night air of the desert, and the occasional bleating from the sheep and goats. She tried to pick out the cry of the ewe in the pain of her lambing, being attended by Abram, but she heard nothing out of the ordinary. Perhaps sheep lambed silently – not like Emtelai whose bellows of pain she had heard years ago. Perhaps the ewe was soothed by Abram's tender murmurings and stroking. Sarai began to cry at the thought of Abram gentling a new lamb into life. She wept in her dark tent until exhausted she finally fell asleep.

It was still dark when she woke and half opened her sore and swollen eyes. A shadow above her added extra blackness to the darkness of the early hours. Abram was crouched beside her bed, motionless as a statue, wrapped in the cloak he had been wearing when he left the tent. He might have only just arrived, but she sensed as soon as she recognised the shadow looming over her that he had been kneeling, hunched above her mattress, looking down, for a long time.

'Abram?' she whispered, more puzzled than afraid.

He looked startled, surprised that she was awake, although he was gazing intently at her when she opened her eyes. He didn't answer. She lifted her hand to his face, just touching the strong broad face she had always loved to stroke for the warmth and reality of him under her palm. She was still barely awake, reaching out for age-old comfort in the night, waking to a weighty chest full of the sobs that sleep had failed to shift. He let her hand lie on his cheek and continued to gaze down at her as if he could not be interrupted in the middle of his thoughts.

'Is the ewe all right?' she asked.

'You've been crying,' he said, and moved his face closer to her to see more clearly.

She reached her other arm up, out from under the cover, and encircled his neck with both her arms as she had done so often before when he bent to kiss her goodnight. And he allowed the pressure of her clinging arms to dip his face closer to her. With their lips no more than a silken thread apart, all was suddenly stillness between them. It was as if they had been struck by some spell that froze their faces together, lips almost touching, him above her, and their eyes locked on each other. They did not breathe, nor move a muscle, but only looked and looked into the eyes that burned with looking into their own. Sarai learned something of desire in that moment, they both learned, conversing silently on the craving that was building from some singular point deep inside each of them, like a glowing spark ready to flame up. They told each other of their passion without words, explained its nature without dialogue, taught and learned the physicality of the flesh without exposition. They held stone still while desire did its work within them, and both of them felt it doubled by the inner longings of the other reaching beyond the boundaries of the skin that had previously kept them separate. They were already making love, static in each other's arms and staring fiercely still into each other's eyes. They learned in that long moment everything the flesh needs to know about being in love. She was wrong about the limitations of love. For a moment, that night, love seemed to have no limitations. All the love in the world, a brother's love, a lover's love, a husband's love, combined and compounded, and she gave herself easily up to it, the simple and obvious arithmetic of love. The first object of her desire would now love her in every way she could and could not yet imagine. What she had longed for, whom she had longed for, now longed for her, and would give himself to her completely. So love was completed by desire, and desire by love, and it seemed so simple. Half-brother, half-husband, half-sister, half-wife becoming wholly love and whole. And she thought that all the ways in which it was possible to love another had come to her that night in the person of her beloved Abram.

And then, as all this fired through her body and mind, she felt the muscles at the back of Abram's neck knot rigid, arresting the downward motion he seemed to be about to make and that she was preparing to rise to receive, and he jerked back from her so suddenly that he had to stand up and totter backwards in order to keep from falling.

He severed the look between them, saying nothing, but using the momentum of his attempt to regain his balance to turn his back on her and fling himself down on his mattress.

The darkness engulfed him like his cloak, and he turned his face to the wall of the tent, to become, to Sarai's stunned eyes, a huddled shadow far off in the unreachable distance.

They were not really wanderers: they had a direction, a final destination. In their own minds, they kept themselves apart from the nomads they encountered along the way, with whom they traded and exchanged.

'Let them think we are like them,' Terah told them. 'But always remember where we have come from and where we are going. We are not desert nomads, we are making a journey. Resettling.' He was adamant about this.

However he thought about himself, Abram turned out to be a talented herdsman. The sheep and goats increased under his care, and if Terah despised this temporarily necessary skill, Abram seemed to immerse himself in it. For Sarai, the business of the days, breaking camp, cooking, moving from well to well, negotiating watering rights with their owners, trading goods with other groups, buying and selling stock, everything was tinged with the thought that when night came, she and Abram would each lie on their separate mattresses in their tent ('This playhouse, fit for children and other such primitives,' Terah observed contemptuously), which for a brief moment she had imagined would become more to her than all the city walls and solid rooms of their life in Ur. The love she had fleetingly glimpsed had had such clarity, like a straight line from familial love to its re-creation. From love to love, she had thought, with a little heartache thrown in by life, just to increase the necessity of remaking love as it was supposed to be. Yes, yes, that simple line turned out to be, in reality, a labyrinth, a confusion of all the knots and tangles of the human heart that two needful, isolated young creatures could not possibly have perceived, let alone unravelled. But why should a time-corrupted palate, requiring a strong sceptical seasoning, no longer beguiled by a simple story of love, see more accurately than thirteen-year-old Sarai in that moment when everything was perfectly clear in the mutual gaze with her beloved? That Sarai fights to retain her innocence. Look at her with knowing, experienced eyes, and she resists, as if what she didn't know then was quite as powerful as what older eyes know now.

There was nothing very unusual about Sarai's failure to conceive by the time they reached Harran. Her periods had not even settled into a regular rhythm, and with the disruption of their flight into exile no one was surprised. It was better anyway for her to grow up some more, they said, childbirth is dangerous to any woman, but at her age the risks were even greater. The body has its own wisdom, Nikkal said. Terah, of course, was in a hurry to secure the continuation of the line, but how could he, who had lost his wife in childbirth, be anything other than patient? Sarai was his daughter as well as his daughter-in-law, and he loved her. There was no great anxiety, and Abram and Sarai were too stunned with the meaning of their intimate separation to speak of it either between themselves or to anyone else. As ever Abram bore the burden of duty and obedience: no ewe or nanny goat ever gave birth without him being in attendance, when Terah called he was there, he never missed the family prayers – but at night he only flung himself on to his mattress when he presumed Sarai was asleep, and rose in the morning before he imagined she would be awake. In fact, Sarai was rarely asleep when he crept into the tent, and usually awake when he left, but the yawning chasm that had opened between them kept her silent. In public, he treated her with the appropriate familiarity and in the tone of a husband for a wife. The years of intimacy they had shared as brother and sister had disappeared overnight, vanished as if they had never been, to be replaced by a shadow-play of marital respect and distance that onlookers assumed concealed the private intimacy of lovers.

Did Sarai's beloved have a proclivity for order and orthodoxy? A distrust of imagination? A slight tendency to pomposity? Perhaps. If these inclinations were not innate, they were certainly instilled in him by the wildly destructive example of Haran. Now, in their wasteland wanderings, in the guilty emptiness of his heart, those qualities hardened like scar tissue.

Sarai ached for lost love, separated from the brother, and outside the family line, and yet not connected to the husband, she was alone in the world, secretly, as she had been when Emtelai died and she had to remain in silence with her private shame. If Abram no longer loved her as a brother, and he could not love her as a wife, she was lost, as distant from belonging anywhere, to anything or anyone, as the cold stars hanging in the desert night ————————

———————— I gave them the Word: live, I told them, and,

of course, they rearranged it. There was no guessing what people would come up with. I looked and saw they had made the vile and the evil in their interaction with each other. From the single us, bad enough, came a larger us. Groups, boundaries, inclusion and exclusion. Just by being plentiful and having the word. None of that existed in my world where eternity and I had rubbed along without disturbing each other. But they had flesh and disobedience, and from the order I had made out of chaos, they had fashioned a chaos of their own, constructed from the deceptions made possible by the juxtaposition of self-consciousness and body. They invented love and lies, and thought themselves giants in the universe.

But from the evil they had produced, I made a deduction of my own: I invented goodness. Again, I was way behind my creatures. They had all the fun on their side. But at least I was learning to function in their oppositional world. It was an attempt to salvage something of my own from that wayward bunch of losers. I needed to find one creature who might represent this new notion in a world devoted to its dialectical opposite. Unfortunately, I had already mingled Enoch, that solitary voice who might have represented goodness if I had thought of it soon enough, so he was unavailable in eternity. I searched and searched and found nothing on earth to match the evil, so I had to make do with good-enough, set about flexing my will.

Noah was nothing special, I have to admit. He wasn't so much good, as I had envisaged it, glorious in his opposition to the filth and fleshiness of his kind, as dull and unimaginative. But I had decided to act, to rid the world of flesh and start again with better material. If he wasn't that special, he was at least better than most. To destroy the world in its entirety would have been to admit that it was badly made. It wasn't. The earth was fine, a lovely working of particles into a coherent whole. I regretted only having made life; that was the source of my pain. My first pain. So I decided that I would begin again with the life on earth, and this time not make from scratch a creature that would think itself into dominion but save one grateful man and his family, who would know to whom they owed their continued, miserable existence. And if in choosing Noah I was to populate the world with dullness, well, so much the better. I had seen enough of the results of autonomy and imagination. Now I wanted obedience.

If nothing else, Noah was that. He didn't once question my intention. He didn't question anything. I spoke, he listened. He didn't query who I might be, but took my word for it when I told him I was his and everyone else's creator, and that I had determined to make an end of all flesh and bring ruin down on a ruined world. I would drown the world and all that was in it, wash away the filth, cleanse it for a new start. Make an ark, with these exact dimensions, I told him, inventing the craft of shipbuilding as I went along and hoping it held water. I will save you and your family, and you will save a breeding pair of each animal I have created, I ordered, indicating in this way, exactly how I regarded the Noahs. It was to be more a prototype of a natural history museum than a lifeboat. Perhaps I was simply too weary to start again from the beginning; and it may be that I had got accustomed to there being something other than eternity.

Noah surpassed himself in lack of imagination. He did not utter a word, he just got on with collecting the gopher wood and reeds. He did not question my decision to destroy all his fellow beings; he did not wonder why he was chosen to be saved. He did as he was told, as smug and stupid as you could wish. When they're not getting above themselves, they're plain servile. If Noah didn't engage my passion the way his arrogant fellows did, at least he boded well for the docility of the future generations he would father. Did I regret wiping out all imagination and creativity in my beings? Perhaps, a little, but at least I would be in charge of creation once again. I would, at last, be ahead of the game. That was the main thing.

Doubts

And they came unto Harran and dwelt there.
GENESIS 11:31

Another beginning. At that time, it was the way of urban living that strangers were given a chance to become (or often enough, re-become), possibly because the other inhabitants didn't care enough about them to stop them, but also because tradition and the past were not as valued as they were by itinerant people. The future is what matters in the town and, of course, the present with its buying and selling, its daily encounters with the familiar and the new, and the sense of remaining while others come and go. People who wanted to stay, provided they were not a financial burden on those already there, helped to sanction the idea of future on which the town thrived.

Harran may not have been the throbbing metropolis of Ur, but it was a busy, bustling town, a crossroads through which traders passed after stopping to make sales and recuperate at the inn, giving and taking news from and to far and wide. If news of the shaming of the family of Shem had reached Harran before their arrival, they were given no indication of it. They sold their livestock, for Abram, Sarai and little Lot, with much regret – Lot wept and Abram wanted to – but greatly to the relief of Terah, who shed years at the sight of solid walls and urban hubbub. Some of the family wealth was converted into brick and labour; a house was built and a workshop, and the group set about becoming members of the community. Once the family had shown themselves to have been only temporary pastoralists, and at ease with the ways of the city, they were welcome enough.

There were, of course, other makers and sellers of icons. Abram had to go slowly, but gradually he was accepted, and his solid, meticulous idols found a market among the wealthier families of the town, those who liked to think themselves more discerning. Terah once again had a courtyard to sit in, and he settled into his daily meditations with relief. Abram chipped and carved to make the same gods he had made in Ur, but with Lot at his side now, instead of Sarai, a new small apprentice who would be the next generation, along with Abram and Sarai's children, in the Shem family business.

This was their new life, as close as Terah and Abram could make it to their old existence. There was nothing to be done about the loss of family members, but they contrived to create a near replica of their former life, just as Abram created images of the old gods. In time, both of those simulations would become subject to intense questioning by Abram, but now all his intensity was taken up with remaking a life for the family to compensate, perhaps, for the new life he was failing to make with his sister-wife.

Sarai regretted the end of their time as travellers. While they were on their way to somewhere, still unsettled, so too was her future. Once they were no longer on the move, the desert wind billowing the walls of their tent and carrying the sound of bleating newborn lambs and kids, when there were no more cool dawn-and-dusk treks, or sweltering days when they sheltered from the blasting sun, too enervated to think clearly; once they were within new solid walls and were where they intended to be, then Sarai's future would be settled, and the loss of brother love and lack of husband passion a fixed reality, not an aspect of a time between. But even after they arrived in Harran, contingency continued to put off the future. The building of walls, the business and new relations took up a great deal of Abram's time, and under Nikkal's guidance Sarai began to learn a woman's household skills, cooking, keeping accounts, spinning and weaving, tending the garden. But at night, she would lie in the room they shared, alone in the bed they did not share, and remember the momentary look between them and then Abram's recoil. The moment when one love was severed and another denied. They should have been, and were supposed by others to be, builders in the night hours too, making a new generation whose home would be Harran, whom they would surround with a wall of love, just as they had known it in Ur. From the ruins of childhood security, they should have been remaking a place of lasting safety for the new children. It was the way of the world. And yet how strange that we have such faith in our notion of the way of the world and how it will continue to operate, when it has already failed to conform to our assumptions of its natural course. Still we suppose that we have only to make an effort to restore normality, as if our courage at putting tragedy behind us and a steadfast vision of how things ought to be will be rewarded by a return to the regular ⸻

⸻ They are incorrigible. You would think having witnessed the death of every living thing on the surface of the earth by drowning (or in the case of the fish, who presented a problem, by steaming – my last-minute solution being to make the rain hot enough to deal with them too), that my only chosen survivors would have devoted themselves to walking in my way, to pleasing me in all things. Initially, doubtless in the throes of relief at standing again on dry land and leaving the foetid enclosure of a box full of animals, Noah showed some gratitude, and made me a delicious burnt offering. I mellowed, thinking things had taken a better turn. I promised never to annihilate life again. Frankly, I realised there was not much point in repeating the procedure. There was an essential flaw in life itself, some reaction between will and flesh that would never be eradicated. I had to admit that what I had made was not perfect. Naturally, when you come to think of it, since only eternity and I am could be that. I would have had to re-create myself to achieve a perfect creature, but I had no wish to share eternity. Either the whole project had to be wiped out, or I had to acknowledge that my plan for a mirror image had gone awry. If I were to see myself in the humanity I had created, I would have to contemplate the differences. Life was defective. It was inherently wayward. I would simply have to settle for this better-than-the-rest remnant I was left with. Noah of the prosaic obedience would have to suffice to repopulate the world. It was the best I could do without admitting out and out defeat.

Yet even the dully dutiful, the unquestioning Noah had a spark of volition, a capacity for the unexpected. Having been saved out of all living things, this chosen one became . . . what? The world's first drunk, that's what. He planted a vineyard, and spent his days tending it and his nights in an alcoholic stupor, like the first old sea-dog that he was, sprawled in his tent, dishevelled, naked with the heat and the drink, so that anyone entering could take advantage of his flabby, exposed flesh. Two of his sons, Shem and Yefet, had the minimal decency to cover him up. The third, Ham, remembered the lascivious ways of his former world and took to practising them on his paralytic old father. Don't ask. These were my chosen ones.

Out of the ruins of the world, Noah, the new Adam, invented the means to get falling-down drunk and his son discovered the joys of taking advantage of the incontinent. I lost all patience. Really, these humans weren't even worth the effort it had taken to make the rain fall. I left them to it, to drink themselves into extinction. Noah didn't notice my absence. He was too entranced by the pretty-coloured rainbows he kept trying to point to in the sky.

I withdrew into myself, and had no plans to take any further interest in the earth and its inhabitants. I was content enough. I was perfect. I was everything. Why should I need anything else? I felt fine, just fine.

In my absence, the creatures had managed quite well to

proliferate, and the sons of Noah, Shem, Ham and Yefet, had had sons of their own who organised themselves into clans and divided up the land between them. It couldn't be long before they were squabbling, and thanks to Cain they had the means to resolve their arguments. It was only a matter of time before humanity solved the problem of its imperfection for me. Yes, I admit I peeked from time to time. But once again I was interrupted by the human voice. This time it was not an Enoch crying out against humanity that caught my attention, but a good deal of shouting and banging. The voices were calling to each other, a chorus of co-operation, if you please, intent for the first time in time itself on a single task. It seemed that I could not even rely on the sons of Cain to bring my little experiment to an end. I should have remembered the power of *us* that I had inadvertently instituted with the splitting of the he/she. And the *us* all spoke the word that I had also given them. They created co-operation and mutual self-interest out of these gifts I had conferred on them, and were using them to plan a lasting monument to their existence. These worms, these ants, these less-than-nothings, whom I had made up in an idle moment of eternity, had devised a future and planned to begin history by planting lasting evidence of themselves. We will be known, they told each other, when we have returned to dust, by those we leave behind. We will be remembered by the future that we have now imagined into being. And they used the very clay from which I had moulded the first he/she to build a visible message to posterity, as they dared to call it.

And again these nonentities took me by surprise. Out of this and that they made something quite new. Give them one thing and they supposed another, then put the two together to make what never existed before. That was my job. Except that I had done it only once, and very practically. These beings I had created invented ideas as well as things. They generalised from the particular. There was none of that before. And I realised that there would be no stopping them now. They threatened to become more and more like me. Perhaps eventually more like me than me. And that was out of order.

But if they had ideas and method, I had raw power, which is not to be underestimated. I confounded their impertinent plan. I couldn't wipe them out. I had given my promise, and that meant I couldn't prevent their ideas, but I could do something about this dangerous ability to co-operate. I had given them the Word and I had given them *us*. Well, then, I would give them many words and a plethora of *us*-es, and then let us see how they would convey their damned ideas and instructions and plans to one another. I baffled them with a multiplicity of words until they could only burble and babble at each other like infants. That took care of that, at least until they invented translation, and even then I'd slowed them down considerably. The opposite of co-operation is division, and soon they wandered away in desultory little groups over the face of the earth. So I began to see that death and future, their inventions, could be my greatest hold over these unruly creatures of mine ————————

———————— For a while, Nikkal continued to tell Sarai not to worry. It was common for young girls at the beginning to take time to settle into the new rhythm of their women bodies and married life. It was even for the best, giving time for her to grow bigger and stronger, better able to withstand the dangers of childbirth. It was the way of the world. Trust it. When the body was ready, she would conceive.

Sarai wasn't worried at first. For her part she was in no great hurry. The most important woman in Sarai's life had died in childbirth. She knew its dangers well. And there was also a thought – more a vague unease – that if she were to be punished for her unnameable feelings about Emtelai's new baby, the time of her own labouring would be most appropriate. And in any case, she knew, though of course she did not say, that it was not just a question of *her* body being ready before she was able to conceive.

All the wanting, and all the resistance to wanting, was in Abram's hands. Love and future depended on him. Sarai could only wait to see how these demands of the world played on his fear of confusion. For that was what he feared, just as it was exactly what Sarai longed for. Where she would have put the parts of love together, Abram strove to keep them separate.

Since that first night they had spoken of nothing but practical matters, and only referred to deeper things in their mutual silence at night. I love you, come to me, come back to me, Sarai would not say. I love you, but I do not know how to love you in all ways, so I will not love you at all, Abram failed to reply. Being old enough did not make him know better. Some things do not become clearer with age and time.

But eventually Abram's craving for conformity and for continuation got the better of his confusion. Gradually, with the silence and emotional separation, his little sister faded from his mind, and Sarai the woman became severed from his past. In order for the direct line of the family of Shem to be assured, it was necessary that Sarai become his wife in deed as well as name. Abram slipped into simplicity and rejected the confusion that had made him reel away from Sarai's willing arms. There was no choice. He had his duty to his family. He had responsibility towards the future.

And so, one night, a full year or more after they were married, Abram once again approached Sarai in her bed.

'Sarai,' he said, touching her gently on her shoulder to waken her. 'We have a responsibility to the future.'

She said nothing. She did not move, apart from opening her eyes.

'Sarai, we are husband and wife.'

Thus assured, Abram bent his face down to her, and this time, completing the move that had been aborted on their wedding night, pressed his mouth firmly against Sarai's. With the tip of his tongue he parted her lips. She gasped at the sudden intimacy and he pulled back a little, not from her, but to look at her face. They had kissed so many times before, so long ago, but there was no pretending that this was like those times.

'Sarai,' he said, and for the first time she heard her name spoken by another like a whispered sigh, a breath of longing. And, as he gently drew back the covers and released the ties that held her nightgown closed, she, again for the first time, felt her body as something other than just a practical concern of her own. She was no beauty, but over the last year or so she had changed from an angular, gawky child into the fresh fleshiness that promised to become womanly. At fifteen now, her breasts were small but shaped and firm, with long, dark nipples, and her belly rounded softly between the dipped curves of her sharp, flared hip-bones. Her face, olive-skinned like the rest of her body, was framed with a tangle of thick black curls. She was on the very edge of childhood, at the boundary of womanhood, young and succulent, careless and awkward still, but full with the promise of ripeness. Like generation after generation, endless generations, they grow, and older eyes comprehend how moving, how desirable is youth on the verge of losing its moment. Beauty or otherwise has nothing to do with it. At that moment, whatever Sarai looked like or might become, she was beauty waiting to be discovered.

It was that which Abram had seen, unwillingly and shockingly, hardly more than a boy himself, after their father told him of the change that he decreed in their relationship. He would suddenly catch himself looking at Sarai, as she caught him, with the eyes of a man instead of a brother. Or half-man, half-brother. He noticed the swell of her breasts, the hint of a nipple, and had wondered how they would feel in the palm of his hand. He had found himself thinking about her thighs and whether the hair between her legs was as dark and thick yet as the hair on her head. He was horrified that with a mere word, one that he had argued against, telling his father that he could only ever see her as a beloved sister, his vision could shift and he could wonder about the secret changes of a child-woman and what they might promise. He was not a virgin. Haran had seen to that back in Ur, taking Abram with him in the early days of his wildness and introducing him to the charms of women who were delighted to induct his young body into the game of sexual pleasure. He had stopped accompanying Haran only when he saw how lost his brother was becoming to his family. But he had experienced the pleasures of gratified flesh, and the memory returned to him, with a greater understanding of the delight the women took in his youthfulness, when Terah announced Sarai was to become his wife.

Now he broke their caress slowly, reluctantly, tearing his eyes away from hers only because of the urgent need to look at her body. He sat back on his heels to get more distance. His hand followed his glance, to her breast, cupping it gently in his palm to feel its substance, and then tracing its contour to arrive at her nipple, which his finger and thumb stroked into a response. She drew in her breath sharply in surprise as she felt that response deep in her abdomen, and he looked up quickly, locating her eyes again to understand what she was feeling. Then he bent and took her nipple in his mouth, sucking on it gently, until the sensation he created in her made her cry out in its delicious strangeness. He continued down her body, kissing her navel and then the small mound above her thighs which parted apparently of their own volition. Abram kissed the inside of one thigh, and then gently ran his bearded cheek along its length, its roughness against her soft flesh almost painful, but something else as well. He sat up again and began to discard his clothes.

'Are you all right?' he whispered.

She nodded, from inside the trance of sensation in which she floated. Again their eyes locked in confirmation of what was happening between them, but this time, she broke the gaze to look at the naked body of her beloved brother and new husband. So dark and strong, so alien and unlike her own small body, Abram was sinew and muscle, rough and solid, covered with body hair where she was smooth, quite other. And although he was not tall, he was massive, ropes of muscle knotted with tension in his thick neck, his shoulders broad, his arms powerful, the arms that had held her so often, strong enough to crush her, or bring comfort to a labouring ewe. She wanted both those things.

He laid himself down beside Sarai on the bed and found the place between her legs with his hand. Once again, after so long, that sudden stillness came over them, a tension between them that made them both hold their breath and seek out each other's eyes. She marvelled that those eyes she knew so well could look at her in such a way. She marvelled at the ease with which his finger found the damp centre of her sex and how welcome it was.

'I'll be very gentle. I won't hurt you,' he said, stroking her slowly.

Soon, when her arms began to tighten around him, he lifted his body over her and kissed her, pushing his tongue gradually into her mouth as he entered her, his penis as delicate as his tongue pressing carefully into her body. When he moved deeper, there was a moment of pain, perhaps only of shock, and she made a single cry. He cried out too, as if the pain and shock were his, and stopped still for a moment, and then something loosened in her and with a moan, hers or his, he was fully inside her. And like a dance they moved together, letting desire play a tune that sang to them of everything they needed to know about their own and the other's pleasure, until with tears and sharp cries they reached a new conclusion.

Apart from her old loving of Abram, now permitted again, Sarai discovered that she loved sex. She perceived the rhythms and transformations it set off within her body. She marvelled at how the physical sensations perfectly, but so differently, echoed her early more generalised feeling of love. As well as being whom she most loved, she discovered Abram as a man. The size and weight of him, the roughness, the hairiness, the smell, pungent and dark, and all that strength containing itself, passionate and careful, big and delicate, surrounding her, inside her. They often stopped moving in the middle of making love and returned to that first still gaze into each other's faces. Their bodies, locked together but not moving, took over, desire whipping around inside them while they simply looked into one another's eyes and felt what was happening to them. His long black hair and broad forehead was wet with sweat, which dripped on her face, and smiling, he broke their gaze briefly, to lick the fallen beads away with the tip of his tongue. She loved his arms around her, clutching her, crushing her almost, the hardness of him, and yet his soft moans and murmurings that matched her climaxes, and something utterly lost as he shuddered into his own and buried his face in her neck.

On this new journey from the past to the future, Abram and Sarai set about expanding their old love into its new form, and it seemed to Sarai as right as anything, that whom each most loved and cherished, whom each was closest to in all the world, should be loved and cherished more, and brought closer still. Their marriage was a transformation of their siblinghood. It seemed to Abram that all memory of their earlier relationship, their sibling relationship, had been buried under their present love. They became, in Abram's eyes, only husband and wife, only lovers, only the pair who would continue the line of Shem. He did not speak about their former life as brother and sister, only about their present passion and future parenthood.

'We will be happy with each other,' he told Sarai, as they lay together, exhausted and drifting towards sleep.

She couldn't imagine any greater happiness. And even then, weak with their love, as she affirmed their happiness by pressing her lips against his neck, desire reasserted itself, and dreamily, half conscious, he entered her again and she received him between her wearied, willing thighs. She still supposed there couldn't be too much love. But then, at that time, she was not yet aware that love was not all there was in the world. So Sarai welcomed what she thought was the return of her beloved Abram's old love for her, not recognising that it was a different thing, with a different purpose: an aspect of something more generalised in him. It seemed right to her. She thought that it was simple. She thought it was what it was.

Nikkal must have spoken to Abram and Terah, because neither of them seemed concerned at Sarai's continuing childlessness at first. A strange thing, this 'at first' which exists only in hindsight. Sarai did not know it was 'at first' at the time. The present has no sequence, no continuation. She simply did not conceive and life went on. There was no moment when she detected that they were entering a new phase, because nothing triggered it as nothing continued to happen, whereas a baby would have begun the next stage in their existence. When nothing happens and goes on happening, it is very hard to know when exactly the nothing happening becomes itself the centre of life.

The baby went on being assumed as a year, and yet another went by. Abram would lie with Sarai after they had made love and run his hand against the flat plain of her belly between the peaks of her rising hip-bones.

'Our child will make you mountainous.'

And they would laugh at the idea of her swelling like one of the ewes.

'But you will be even more beautiful.'

Sarai wasn't so sure.

Then the time came when Abram's hand hovered on her stomach as if he were trying to feel the heat of a new life within; and then as if he were willing that new life into being. And by then Nikkal received Sarai in her tent each new month for her menstrual seclusion with a slight sigh.

'Perhaps next month,' she would say, no longer adding that it was perfectly natural.

Still, it was known that some women were slow to conceive but eventually got pregnant. It was a delicate thing. It was also known, though no one spoke of it, that some women were barren, and then all the herbal concoctions that Nikkal infused for Sarai would be no use at all. Even so, Sarai could not say even three years after they had married that she was terribly alarmed, happy as she was to be fully a wife now to Abram, or even that she sensed excessive concern from the others at her failure to produce a child. They were all waiting, but in the present tense of living, waiting presupposes the arrival of what we are waiting for. It is only in retrospect that we know for certain that it was never going to come.

Some part of Sarai felt great relief at the lack of change, but change came none the less, though it too was not obvious at the time, only later. We are all haunted by the ghost of the present as we recollect the long distant past, so clear now in its shifts and phases. The present lives alongside our sweep of memory, all unknowing about its own nature, existing minute by minute, wondering if this means something, or that signifies something else, but unable to grasp the nature of its own time. All the while the present has its own past to look back to, but there is no guidance in it, submerged as it is by the present now. Only when it's all over, when it's too late, can you know for sure that *then* marks the change that altered the course of a life. The present is blind. Just as well, I suppose. What was there to do about anything at the time? But what is there to do about anything when all is said and done?

Understand, they were a long time in Harran. A very long time. For Abram, Sarai and Lot, it was their home for much longer than Ur had been. They lived the best part of their lives there. The longest part, I mean of course by that strange turn of phrase, referring purely to time: who can say for sure, even in retrospect, that then and not later was truly the best part of their lives? They lived the easiest part of their lives in Harran, easier than it was to become, that much is sure. But let us acknowledge that the easiest may not necessarily be the best. Sarai did not know that the worst of times were to come, but there were moments, too, later on, that perhaps she would not have missed. Not many, but some, probably. So years passed into decades, and youth into middle years.

Eventually the time came when Abram stopped talking to Sarai about the children they would have. If his hand hovered over her belly now, it was for the sensual pleasure of feeling its silkiness against his rough work-hardened fingers, and later, perhaps, silently noticing the work the passage of time had wrought on her no longer taut, no longer so silky flesh. They continued for many years with their life, and in spite of the lack of children and the workings of time and habituation, they remained, remarkably, lovers and in love. Sarai knew that there were discussions and then arguments with Terah. Once again she heard voices raised in her father's rooms. Later she learned that Terah was insisting that her husband take a concubine, that it was his duty to produce an heir. Not that her father loved her any less as his daughter, but his plans for Sarai as a daughter-in-law had not worked out, and the future of the family of Shem was playing on his mind. It was certainly playing on Abram's mind, but it was not only love for Sarai that stopped him from taking a new wife. He was as dutiful a husband as he was a son. He was too loyal to Sarai, to the idea of *wife*, to accede to Terah's demands. And if Sarai's relationship with him shifted once again, it might bring back to mind the nature of their former relationship. It would have been quite normal for him to find a woman to have his children, yet he balked, even though his desire for offspring and the securing of the line was quite as strong as Terah's. He perceived himself as a one-woman man, Sarai's Abram, quite out of his time, when a man might reasonably have a multiplicity of women. It was his nature to choose and stay with one woman, one lover, one friend. Perhaps that was all he could cope with. But he felt that he must remain committed and devoted to a single other, and in a world where wives were repudiated not just for failing to bear children but for having an aesthetically displeasing cast in one eye, Sarai appreciated this trait in her singular and remarkable man. So Abram chose Sarai instead of posterity, and the dissent between him and Terah grew.

Still the marriage was barren. As the decades passed, they continued to love each other, and were as close as any brother-sister, husband-wife had ever been, and yet from such closeness no children emerged. It never once occurred to her or anyone else that it might be Abram who was unable to have children. But, of course, Sarai's inability to conceive was at the back of her mind a punishment, perhaps, after all, worse than dying in childbirth, for her long-ago guilty resentment of Emtelai's happiness. The notion that her thoughts had contributed to those deaths had not disappeared with the passing years. She deserved not to have children.

So the years accumulated behind them. They became as settled and respected a family as they had been in Ur, the business thrived and nothing this time broke the thread of their lives. Terah aged further into his silent contemplation in the courtyard, and Abram's glossy black hair became speckled with grey, and the skin at the corners of his eyes criss-crossed with time. Sarai aged too. Her waist thickened, her breasts were no longer firm, her thighs no longer taut. Yet she saw in her glass that the girl she had been, who was no beauty but was desirable for her sheer youth, had aged into a handsome woman. Abram's desire for her did not diminish, and her appetite for him remained. His strong, compact body still felt good beside her. And they knew all the better how to pleasure each other. They were companions by day and each other's comforter at night. They no longer made love in the hope of producing children, Sarai knew, but for and to each other. Their childlessness was never spoken of, but it made their caresses all the more tender. He was a good man. She couldn't have asked for better. And if she had failed him as a bearer of children, she was, he often told her, everything, everything a man could ever hope for in a lifelong friend and wife. Abram did not want any other woman, however much Terah said it was his duty, and she could not bring herself to pretend that the idea of his lying in anyone's arms but hers would not break her heart.

Eventually, Lot grew into a fine young man, with his father's fair good looks and a winning smile. As Abram continued to refuse to take another woman, Terah turned to Lot, for all the unsatisfactoriness of his paternity, and found him a wife. This time Terah was not betting his future on a slip of a girl. Lot's wife was a big-hipped sturdy woman in her middle twenties, no beauty by anyone's standards, which accounted for her availability at such an age, but as fecund-looking as a nanny goat in heat. It was impossible not to imagine her heavy, bouncing breasts dripping milk, or her great thighs parting with easy regularity to allow babies to slip into the world like eels through a net.

'Looks aren't everything,' Terah assured the alarmed young Lot. 'We need a baby-maker. Make the babies and you can have all the beautiful young concubines you can cope with.'

Lot did not have the innately dutiful character that his uncle Abram possessed and which, paradoxically, had caused him to reject Terah's wishes, but he was not a strong-minded young man. Perhaps the shadow of his unmentionable father weighed on him and made him fearful. He was too willing to please, too tentative to argue his case. Terah had always been hard with him, fearing, perhaps, that he might have inherited Haran's waywardness. But if Haran was a wild young man, Lot, for whatever reason, was tame. He married his prodigious bride and set about making babies. When they came they were girls, not quite what was wanted, but the pressure on Abram was lessened a little. At least there was a chance of sons of Shem to come.

If Lot's babies eventually took some of the pressure away from them, it was still hard for Abram and Sarai to see them feeding hungrily from their mother's breast, and growing into their own young lives. Sarai was fond of them, but their very existence was a reminder of what she could not do. Abram and Sarai let silence bear the strain of their disappointment at having no heirs of their own. She had managed to submerge her guilt deep into the recesses of her mind, and it seemed as if Abram had come to terms with the situation. In fact, in his monumentally patient way, it turned out that Abram was only waiting until all hope was extinguished before allowing his despair to emerge and change the course of all their lives, just when it had come to seem that their lives had been all but said and done.

It wasn't until several months after Sarai's periods had stopped coming that Abram began to exhibit behaviour that caused her anxiety. Eventually he noticed that she no longer slept apart from him each month. Men do not keep an internal calendar as women are inclined to do.

'Is it over?' he asked one night, resting his bearded cheek against her belly after they had finished making love.

'For months now,' she told him, caressing his hair, fully grey now, but still thick enough to please her raking fingers.

He was silent for a moment.

'Now there can be no surprises,' he said, and turned his face full into the flesh of her stomach.

She heard this with wonder.

'Abram,' she said, lifting his head to look into his face. 'After all this time, did you still hope there would be?'

'No, no, of course not.'

He brought himself back to lie face up beside her.

'But you said . . .'

'I suppose there was always a faint chance that something might happen, just the possibility. I don't mean I was expecting . . . only now there can be no chance . . .'

'All this time?' She was astonished. 'All this time, and you still thought we might have a child.'

He was uncomfortable. 'No, not really. Not exactly *thought*. It's just that now all possibility is over. I suppose, you never know, you can't be sure that something won't happen, not until now, not until it's too late for anything . . .'

Sarai had had no idea. She had known there would be no child after the first years. She had learned to greet the sight of each monthly flow with a grim nod of recognition of how things are, not with bitter disappointment. Her monthly period existed merely to mock her infertility. But that was better than to feel, month by month, year after year, that the blood washed away another lost child, another life that her body had failed to make, that her arms would never hold, breasts nourish, lips kiss, eyes feast upon. To have had to experience such loss every month after the first number of years would have drained her of her own life. She took her menstrual blood to be a discharge of a faulty mechanism, no more capable of sustaining life than an empty sack. She came to know deeply that she did not have the ability to nourish new life. Barrenness was the nature of her interior, and to hope that it might change each month, and to have that hope dashed with deadly regularity would have made her quite mad. Abram's love for her exterior body was all that had prevented her from hating herself utterly. It gave her the right to exist. Yet now it seemed that each month, for all these years of months, *he* had hoped and suffered disappointment.

And now, for all the pain she realised he must have felt, Sarai burned with anger.

'How could you?' she shouted at him, and began to beat his chest with her clenched fists. 'How dare you? How could you have hoped all this time?'

Abram had no idea why she should be screaming and flailing at him, and nor, at that moment, did Sarai, but she could not stop. The tears streamed down her face as she hit out and tore at him with her nails in such rage that he had to grasp her wrists to stop her drawing blood. And even then her anger was so powerful that she broke free and scored his cheek and chest with bloody scratches. They had had arguments over the years, but never had she been so incandescent, so beyond control. Abram was afraid of what he saw. Instead of trying to take her wrists again, he enclosed Sarai in his arms, clutching her raging body tightly against his so that she could do nothing more than writhe against him.

'Stop, stop, stop,' he called out to her, in a tone that begged rather than ordered. He sounded fearful, confused, but for long minutes she was unable to do anything except fight against him to break free so that she could gouge at his flesh and scream at him. It came from nowhere, but took her over entirely, and Abram could only hold her firm next to his beating heart until eventually, from sheer exhaustion, her screams transformed into deep sobs and her fight subsided into despair.

Only very occasionally do we understand that the years which seemed in their passing to have been easy enough to live through in fact have accumulated, accreted like scar tissue, and made a difference to our very substance. Without that chance remark by Abram, Sarai might have lived and died without knowing that each second, each dismissed thought, each suppressed anxiety changes who you were from what you might have been to who you are. An obvious discovery once it is made, even back in those days, but still she managed to live through the decades of her childhood and middle age until that moment, in the unexamined belief that life was time passing, and something external to the one who lived it. Now, when she might most reasonably be subsiding into the final portion of her existence, she discovered in her unaccountable rage all the moments of the earlier decades vivid within her as if, at last and all at once, they were jostling for a last-minute recognition.

She was, by the standards of the times, quite old now, and by any standards beyond her reproductive purpose as a woman. What was she doing beating and screaming at her even more elderly, devoted husband, when until then she had been all silence, appreciation and acquiescence? It was unseemly, at the very least, to say nothing of pointless. What had Abram done to deserve the marks she had scored on his body? From her madness and fury she screamed an answer, one that, in the excitement, neither of them recognised as the plain truth.

'All wasted, all wasted,' she howled at him, as he held her close in his clutches. 'Your damned obedience, your wretched dutifulness, your devotion has wasted our lives. How could you do this to me? In the name of love, how could you condemn me to this half-life, this pretend world we made of love and nothing else? How could you have not cried out all this time? You never wept on my naked bosom. We never wept and raged together. You are not loyal. You're a traitor.'

They both thought she was babbling insane nonsense. Neither of them paid much attention to the meaning of what she shouted, only to the state she was in. But after the rage had subsided, in the days and nights of what seemed to be restored normality, her words came back to her and demanded her attention. She was shocked at the anger she discovered, so powerful as to seem, that night, entirely to possess her. Abram was shocked also, but he feared Sarai was ill. *Her* shock was at discovering she was someone quite different from who she thought she was, that she was someone who in a long, contented enough life, had never spoken before. Where once *the way of the world* had sufficed as explanation for what and how she and everything was, now it had become her gaoler and her enemy: the dark deviser of her acquiescence and unconsciousness of her own self. And Abram, her beloved, was complicit in the crime of wasting both of their lives.

She did not have any precise notion of what an unwasted life might have been. It was not that she perceived several options she had failed to take. The way of the world was too powerful to allow such imaginings. But it was enough to discover that she was getting old, getting near the end, at least at the point where nothing new was going to happen ('Now there can be no surprises'), only more or less much the same, and that there might have been other ways of living or thinking or being. It didn't matter that she couldn't conceive of them, what mattered was that she understood there were unsuspected possibilities, when all along she had been led to believe, allowed herself to believe, that there was only one life to be led: the one that she lived in. Even her inner rage seemed a precious new discovery, an alternative to the suppressed guilt and unfulfilled hopes that had led her life by the nose since she was a tiny child. Perhaps it was no one's fault. Of course it was no one's fault, but one of the revelations of that wild attack on Abram was the satisfaction she felt at unfairly and unreasonably blaming him. The very unfairness and irrationality of her accusations gave her a sense of freedom such as she had never experienced before ————————

———————— Irrationality! Oh, yes, irrationality. Who could have foreseen such a trait? It should have been so simple. I give life, and life, in gratitude and in order to continue, does what its creator wants. In the end, it was not disobedience itself that was the cause of the problem between me and my creatures right from the beginning, it was irrationality: a rogue tendency that arrived like a virus out of nowhere. A – believe me – unintended corollary perhaps to the great big brains I had bestowed on them to think me with. A side effect of complexity, I suppose. And what rational being could have suspected the accident of irrationality? It was their capacity to risk everything for no good reason at all, for the sheer pleasure of the unreason of it, that was the cause of the disobedience in the first place. How could I, pure reason, deal with that? Disobedience I could punish, but what could I do about the irrational? It made no sense to me. It seems so straightforward: don't eat of that tree or you will be punished. Punishment is bad. Life is good. Carry on doing what you are doing and it will go on being good. What reasonable being would disobey? Human being. For me the strangeness of my creation had been the incidental invention of consequence, but these piffling creatures did not just embody consequence, they even chose to ignore it. Got above themselves, and were always trying to get above me.

I admit to a loss of confidence. A feeling of lowered self-esteem. I could have retired into eternity, but always at the back of my mind was the troubling fact of the continued existence of my creation. It wasn't just my promise to Noah – though my word was *my* word and if I didn't keep it, it would become theirs – that stopped me from destroying the whole shebang. It was my own sense of failure. How could *I am* fail? Where would that leave me? I resolved to try once more, but this time to infiltrate humanity with my kind of human being. I would start small and build my kingdom on earth from within. I searched the world for another Noah, but this time a solitary, needful one whose history I could develop and control. I remembered that death and future were my chosen weapons. Once again I took what I had learned from my creatures whose life-spans were mere puffs of existence compared to my eternity. Now I would use cunning to make the world I wanted. Time, after all, was on my side ————

———— Nothing changed immediately after Sarai's outburst and her new understanding of her life. Not so that it could be noticed. When morning came, Abram looked at her nervously, but she shook her head in reassurance that the tempest was past. Only the scratches on Abram's face and chest remained to show that anything had happened the night before. But it had happened, both Abram's realisation and her own. The scratches on each of their souls did not heal and could not be explained away as an accident in the workshop.

From that moment there was the beginning of a distance between them that had never existed since the troubled days at the beginning of their marriage. Neither of them was aware of it at first. They carried on as old friends and old lovers, but some part of Sarai remained separate, as if a new place within her had been created on that night, a place of seclusion that Abram could not penetrate with either love or familiarity. From then on there was the way of the world, which was lived as it had to be lived, but there was also a new inner world of Sarai's own, where the way of the world was called into question, where question followed question, where ready answers had no authority and dissatisfaction provided secret satisfactions of its own. It was tentative at first, but she began to get the hang of it gradually, and soon found it possible to exist in both worlds simultaneously. In her interior world, Sarai began hesitantly to dance and to discover that the tune the world played was not the only one.

And it must have been then, too, that Abram began an inner journey of his own, though being Abram his steps would have been slow and I do not think he heard a tune at all. Yet it was he, not Sarai, whose steps eventually led outside himself to clash with the world and its ways. One should never underestimate the unimaginative, and their stolid power, once trouble has colonised their minds, to wreck havoc on the world.

At first it seemed only that there was a new quality of brooding to his usual quietness of manner. Abram was always a doer rather than a sayer or a thinker, but Sarai began to notice a strained look on his creased and usually tranquil face. He had been easy in his silence. Yet now she was reminded of the dark, pained adolescent who had been her briefly troubled brother not yet come to terms with the approach of manhood. Sarai had quite forgotten him. It shook her that that clumsy, reaching boy and her husband were still one and the same. She wondered if her father's troubles were taking hold in Abram. Terah's bouts of madness had long since been transformed into a permanent gloom, so that Sarai hardly remembered his sudden disappearances and the tears behind closed doors. And yet her observations of her husband could have been nothing more than an over-observant wife making too much of a passing mood that anyone might fall prey to. He was gentle with her, but more inclined to hold her close than make love, and as he held her, she felt more and more that his arms clung to her while his mind pulled against the comfort and tried to draw away.

'Is something troubling you?' she asked one night.

'No,' he replied, too fast, too harsh.

She realised her strange behaviour the night he asked her about her periods had frightened him. Whatever was going on, he hardly dared to share it with the one person he was closest to for fear that he might cause another storm. Part of Sarai felt dismay at the wedge she had placed between them, but she was still exhilarated by the new space inside herself and her unreasonable anger at the reasonableness of her husband.

After some moments, he whispered, 'We are growing old.'

'Yes, my dear, we are.'

'Sarai,' he tried. 'Sarai, I don't know what it is for. When it is all over, what is left? What sense . . .?'

She felt her heart lurch towards him, but she ignored it and did not reassure him. She refused to build a bridge over which he might have brought his troubles safely to her.

'It is all for nothing,' she said.

His troubles, she guessed, were much the same as her own, and yet their understanding of what it meant to each of them was crucially different, and this encouraged Sarai's silent anger. Their failure to have children, and his realisation that it was now too late for her to bear them was not, like hers, a sense of part of herself denied, but a sudden and urgent recognition of his own mortality. Perhaps in the end both their interpretations amounted to the same thing, but his focus was more sharply on his own extinction, as if it had never really occurred to him before. His crisis was the newly certain knowledge that he was going to die. Sarai, too, knew that she was going to die, though she was not so taken by surprise by the thought, but for her, childlessness meant that she would die without having had the experience of holding her child in her body, her infant in her arms, and discovering the full capacity of her woman's body. Well, we all have our own concerns, our own interpretations of the meaning of time passing. Perhaps Abram's were more honest, more direct. But it angered Sarai that it took the end of her periods to open Abram's mind to such thoughts.

'Let's sleep,' she said. 'There is nothing to be done.'

But Abram had awoken. Abram, who had sleepwalked through the decades, through the way of the world, doing everything he was supposed to do, doing everything he could to wrench life back to the normal without wondering about the point of it all: that Abram had been shaken awake and his mind teemed with unaccustomed and disturbing thoughts. For him too, at last, the way of the world had lost its transparency. And though Sarai felt it strangely after a lifetime of loving care and comradeship, part of her was not sorry for his torment.

His brooding and silence deepened after that until the day when Lot raced through the house to find her.

'Something's the matter with Abram,' he panted, pointing wildly in the direction of town, his face a picture of distress.

Sarai had a sudden vision of her brother Haran and the blood pouring from his throat. In that second, she experienced a lifetime of regret for her coldness towards Abram. But he was not dead.

'A woman came to the shop and ordered a statue of Nanna,' Lot explained breathlessly. 'Abram was back in the workshop. I heard him chipping away, but when she spoke, the chipping stopped and he came into the shop holding the half-made block of stone and his chisel. "Why?" he asked her. Well, barked at her. I've never heard him speak like that to anyone, let alone a customer. I thought perhaps she owed us money. But even so. She was confused. "What?" she asked, looking at him and then looking at me. "I said, 'Why?'" He actually shouted at her. She was quite frightened, and so was I. Abram looked so . . . fierce. Can you imagine? But she said, "My daughter is to marry and she'll need the god for her new household." Abram went right up close to her and waved the block of stone in her face. He had hardly started work on it, just chipped away a bare outline. "We do not sell gods," he bellowed into her face. "We sell lumps of stone." No one knew what to say. "Look," he shouted. "Does this look like a god to you? Do you want to pray to this? Go on, get down on your knees and pray to it for many grandchildren. Ask it to stop the sun coming up in the morning and going down at night. Offer it libations of your most precious oils, sacrifice your finest, fattest kid in front of it, and ask it to keep you alive until the end of time. Go on. Kneel!" The poor woman wanted to run, but she was too afraid of Abram. He wrenched her hands away from her mouth and dropped the unfinished statue into them. "Here, it's yours. How could a person sell a god? I give it to you. There!" The woman looked down at the object in her hands and said, "But this is just a block of stone. I want a statue for my daughter and her husband to worship." He screamed, "What kind of fool are you to worship a statue?" I swear, Sarai, he said that. "Why should I bother carving and shaping? Go home and worship a lump of stone. In fact, if I can turn a rough mass of stone into a god with my bare hands, you should worship *me*. Why don't you bend your knee to me? In future, I'll carve statues of myself. I'm the one with the power to transform inanimate nature into deity." I just stood there. I couldn't believe what I was seeing and hearing, and from *Abram*. I couldn't move. I hardly dared breathe, I tell you. Then Abram threw down the chisel and stormed out of the shop. I did my best to smooth things out with the woman, I was terrified she would go to the temple and tell the priests. I said that Abram had had a fever for a couple of days and that he had come into work delirious when he should have been at home being tended. She was terribly shocked, but what had happened, what he had said, was so dreadful that she was inclined to believe me. I placated her as much as I could and promised her a statue, a fine statue, free of charge. And she went away. But even if she doesn't report it to the temple, she's sure to talk about it. What shall we do, Sarai? What's the matter with him? Did he come back here? Have you seen him?'

Lot finally halted his outpouring of alarm and tears of panic sprang to his eyes.

Sarai could hardly take it in. She spoke only to his final question.

'No, he isn't here.'

It seemed to her as if her sudden flashing memory of Haran had not been so far off the mark. A terrible shudder of fear went through her.

'Quickly, we must go to the temple. He'll be there.'

'Shall I speak to Terah?' Lot asked, relieved to be receiving instructions at last, but wishing to be excused from finding Abram.

'No, don't speak to anyone. Come with me.'

They ran towards town, until they came into the busy street that led to the temple, and then they slowed to a speedy walk, not wanting to alert the townspeople to their alarm. They found Abram at the back of the cavernous space of the temple, standing, leaning against a pillar, almost casually, absolutely still. His hand rested thoughtfully on his beard, his eyes were fixed on the worship of a small family group at one of the shrines nearest to him. He looked calm, but utterly engaged, as if he were studying, or solving a problem in his head. Anyone else seeing him there might have supposed he was looking at his handiwork – the statue being worshipped was his own – and considering, seeing it *in situ*, whether it needed further refinement. As Sarai looked at him, she wondered if Lot and not Abram had been over-come by a fit of madness. But she knew better.

She went up to him, signalling for Lot to wait where he was. 'Abram?' she said, touching his sleeve.

He turned to look at her, not at all alarmed. 'This is all nothing,' he said, almost lightly. There was even a small smile playing on his lips. 'Nothing at all.'

'Let's go home and talk about it.'

He shrugged and let Sarai lead him out of the temple. It seemed his business there was finished anyway.

She sent Lot back to the shop and told him not to talk to anyone about what had happened. He was delighted to get away.

Back in their room, Abram flung himself down on the bed, as if he were exhausted. 'There is nothing,' he mur-mured, the lightness gone now from his voice.

'What?' she asked, and he looked up sharply at her, sitting beside him, as if it were the first time that he had noticed her there. After a moment, he seemed to make up his mind to take her into his confidence.

'There is nothing, Sarai.' His voice was hollow, dully hor-rified, his eyes blank, his strong body prostrate as he spoke. 'We are born and we die. Nothing else. The rest is emptiness.'

'Well, we do some living in between.'

'For what? We work to feed ourselves. That is all. Beyond that it is all pretence. Beyond that we just try to cover up the truth that we are no more than another herd of animals. Eating, sleeping, working. It's true that we can think, but we choose comfort rather than thought. I know what happened to Haran,' he said, with a sudden urgency. 'I know why he did what he did. But it's taken so long for me to understand. My whole life. A whole lifetime of lies. We live a lie from birth to death. We're no better than the ants, but we pretend to ourselves that there is something more. That there are gods who make things happen, who are concerned with us, who are our makers and masters who we can placate and persuade. When, after all, there is no reason, no purpose, no point in anything. There is no placating nothingness. Sarai, we are accidental creatures living accidental lives. And everything we have surrounded ourselves with, gods, priests, commerce, family, all of it is to mask the fact that we live, we die and nothing matters.'

As she listened to her middle-aged, newly tormented husband, a sense of familiarity came over Sarai that at first she couldn't place, until she remembered herself as a young child alone in her bed in the dark, with these very same thoughts going through her head. She would think of Terah and Emtelai near by, and her brothers and of how she belonged to them, but then she would recall that she only nearly belonged to them, that by some accident she had been born to another mother, a woman without a name. And following this thought was the possibility that she might have been born into an entirely different family. Beggars, perhaps, or courtiers. The arbitrary nature of who she was had gripped and terrified her, and sent her mind out from the safe room where her loved ones surrounded her, to the lonely dark night, a black horizon, the endless sky, the moon hanging heavy in the darkness, and soon not just she but everything seemed quite accidental, and she sensed we were all lost, even adults, in a vast black purposeless place. That we only seemed to belong where we happened to be, but that really we were just dotted about the earth like dust motes revealed in sunlight. When this panic took hold of her, she pulled her mind back urgently to the comfort of her bed, and the sounds of her home and her family around her, but the damage had been done, and she knew that it was all a charade, and that underneath the belonging, and in spite of the wall of love, was wasteland and wandering. She tried to think about the gods, and how they had ordered the world and formed the earth and sky, and looked down at all with pleasure or anger that resulted in the shape of their lives. But she knew it was nonsense. A story for children. Deeply, she knew that those gods didn't really exist. But, terrible though it was, the terror of this thought was less than the fear that all her loving connections were human-made consolations for the emptiness that actually existed. That perhaps everyone knew of the emptiness, even adults, but they pretended they didn't, and shored up their fears with fantasies of purposefulness. Sarai was a child, none of these words could come, but the images, the feelings were stark and irrefutable – at least in the dead of night – and she struggled, when they came to her, to return to her former understanding of the world that was being wrenched away from her. It never worked. She was saved only by her childish body grabbing at sleep, and in the morning light, her fears were put away, not even remembered until the next time they occurred.

Sometime in the process of growing up, of living in the way of the world, these thoughts had stopped, but now, as

Abram spoke, she realised that he was voicing exactly those childhood terrors of hers. After a lifetime of inhabiting a world that was self-evident to him, he was asking the questions that only a child foolishly dared to ask, and which it seemed some children, like Haran, couldn't give up asking.

Sarai spoke aloud, voicing her reflections, though not clearly, 'These are children's thoughts.'

Abram misunderstood and took it that she was dismissing his anxieties when she was only recollecting how she had herself experienced them. He looked at her sharply.

'You are all I have ever had in the world,' he said, as if she, like the gods, had been discovered to be an illusion.

'No, Abram, I meant only that we must live our lives in the world. That the stories we tell about it make living possible. Look at what happened to Haran. It doesn't matter what is real and what isn't, so long as we are able to continue. And you and I *do* have each other. We have made and lived a life together.'

Sarai spoke these words to her distraught husband as, just days ago, he might have spoken them to her when she was distressed, and discovered the nonsense and lies that she had been living. Why didn't she confirm his fears and tell him that she, too, shared them? That the way of the world tasted to her, too, of ashes? She told herself she was doing a kindness to Abram, attempting to soothe his fears, but there was cruelty in her rejection of his vision, a refusal to let him know he was not alone. Her lifelong love, her husband. She used the way of the world, which she had learned to despise, to punish him. For what? For being her love and not her teacher, perhaps.

'Our life together will end for each of us in nothingness,' Abram groaned. 'We will die, and everything we have known and have discovered and learned will be lost. We might as well not have lived.'

'But since we have lived, we have lived happily enough together,' she persisted.

'Yes, we've made the best of it,' Abram's voice was grey with despair, 'but when it ends there will be nothing. Nothing will remain.'

'No children, you mean.'

'No future. No one even to recite our names before the gods.'

'Recite our names to the gods who do not exist?'

He turned and looked very hard at her.

'You're not surprised at what I said. You're not even shocked.'

She became angry again at the self-absorption of this man she had loved for a lifetime.

'Do you think I hadn't thought about death, about child-lessness, about the way life has been arranged or worse not arranged by . . . by . . . whatever it is, but not us? Perhaps, after all, the years we've been together *do* mean nothing. Do you think only you think? What took you so long to get around to such thoughts? And now you've had them, you can conclude like me that life must be got on with. And that the future is none of our business. Anyway, no one has ever recited *my* name in the begettings, and nor would they. I would have been forgotten soon enough after my death, even if we had had children.'

She tasted her bitterness and almost envied his despair.

He took her by the shoulders and shouted, as if to drown out her words, 'I can't bear it!'

She shouted back, 'You must bear it! We must all bear it. That is all that there is to be done.'

He began to shake Sarai, but stopped suddenly.

'No,' Abram said, shaking his head fiercely. He rose from the bed and abruptly left her in their room, to wonder what this new turmoil in their lives would bring.

Abram was gone for three days. Sarai told Terah that he had gone to a new quarry he had heard about to see if he could improve the quality of the stone they were using. In the meantime, just as in the times of her father's disappearances, Sarai sent the household servants into the desert to search for him. It seemed that they were all implicated in the family madness. Only Lot remained unburdened by intolerable thoughts, but only, Sarai sometimes suspected, because he had no thoughts at all. He was amiable and always did what he knew was expected of him, but there was something quite insubstantial about him, as if he were hollow. At least he did not seem to suffer like the rest of them. He knew very little about his father's trouble and had never asked for the details of his death. But it had always hung in the air, just as Haran's unspoken name hovered like a cloud above the lives of the family of Shem. The slightness of Lot's personality in this family of strong and brooding men and secretly troubled women (Sarai wondered now, had Emtelai been troubled? But of course she had, with Terah as a husband), was perhaps his only way of surviving the terrible facts of his birthright. But his daughters seemed sunny enough, so there was a chance that this would be the escape route for their apparently doomed family. Sarai began to think it might be just as well that Abram and she had borne no children. Perhaps there was purpose in it, after all.

They could not conceal the truth from the aged Terah for long. After three days, Abram returned of his own accord. He burst, filthy, coated in dust, into the courtyard where Terah sat in his habitual meditation. Sarai had just come to suggest Terah take an afternoon nap. Abram ignored her and dropped to his knees beside his father. If Sarai had seen him on the street in town, she would not have recognised her husband. It was not just his torn clothes and dirt-encrusted face, nor his tangled and matted hair, dusted dull with sand. His eyes gleamed as if a fire had been lit behind them, and their lids and rims were sore and red, seeming indeed to have been burned with its heat. Abram buried his head in Terah's lap and began to sob like a small child.

'I'm lost, Father,' he wept. 'There's nothing but blackness. I am in my grave and the earth is piling on top of me. Father, I can only see . . . nothing, black emptiness.'

Terah stared down for a long moment at his son wetting his robe with tears, crying out in anguish. Then he lifted up his hands, holding them high, away from Abram's bent head, avoiding contact, shrinking back in his chair, trying to disengage himself from the burden in his lap.

'Again?' he moaned, pressing further back into the chair, his hands still rigidly aloft. 'Again?'

Abram felt the tension in Terah's body, and the absence of his father's consoling hands. He lifted his head and eyes to look up at him. 'Father? Help me.'

Terah did not move, but looked down at Abram as if he were seeing a ghost. 'Will it never end?' he cried out.

Sarai ran to Abram and pulled him away from Terah, murmuring sounds of comfort, words, she supposed, though she hardly knew which. She manhandled him as gently as she could out of the courtyard and into the house, aware all the while of Terah needing her attention too, pulled between the two devastated men. She got Abram to their room and left him weeping helplessly on the bed. Then she ran back to the courtyard, calling out to the servants to help her with Terah whom she found with his head lolled back and tears of old and new grief streaming silently down his face.

For several days Sarai and the rest of the household attended to the necessary details of life: Lot saw to the business, his wife and daughters took care of the children, and Sarai managed the day-to-day running of the household, glad to have practical tasks to think about while coming and going along corridors that echoed with the inconsolable weeping of the two men in their separate rooms.

Between our own needs and the needs of others lies routine. A servant kept a constant watch on Abram, who had spent his tears and now lay silently on their bed, staring into his void. Yet another servant ministered to Terah, whose tears continued to flow. Sarai ran the household with a fervour borne of a terror of standing still. At night, however, she had no choice but to lie beside Abram, who barely registered her presence. She was tired of thinking, of fearing the future and trying to penetrate the past for clues. She discovered a capacity for sleeping through Abram's wakeful agony, but before she slept, and in the morning when she woke, there was a period when reflection forced itself on her, and then she found herself filling with rage at the weeping, will-less men of her house. The bleakness that paralysed Abram and Terah was no less for Sarai. She felt pitiless, so every morning she threw back the cover and devoted herself to the efficient management of a household that had come to a halt. Either that, or she should take her own despairing place next to Abram and they could all rot into dust.

Lot could not comprehend any of it. For one thing, he had only half the story, having been deprived of the facts of the family's past, and for another he could not conceive of the depths to which Abram and Terah had sunk, having no place like that lurking in his own mind. Lot's world skittered along on the surface, and Sarai, for one, at that time, thanked the gods for it. At least someone in the household was shallow enough to get on with it.

And what of Sarai's lifelong love for Abram, her brother, her husband, her friend? Don't ask. She took very great care not to ask the question of herself at the time. The answer might have finally sent her spiralling down into his helpless condition. With the acquisition of the long view, we do not demand such black and white statements of our emotions. We allow abeyance. But then, to have answered the question in what seemed like an honest way would have been to toxify all her past as self-deception, as meaningless. All that love, and now . . . Easy to be so much older and wiser, when life is all but past and there is no future to fear, no body that once filled us with love lying inert and unavailable next to us. It is easy to be gentle with ourselves once all of it is history. Beware the wisdom of the old, it is devoid of life ————————

———————— I had had my fill of mankind and its seething, fleshy, unreliable ways. My new plan was to focus on just one man from whom I could create the future and history both, slowly and at my own pace, so that this go round, I would be ahead of the game. *I am* would become *I will be*: an *I am* with a future. I was getting the hang of time.

Abram was ideal for my purpose. The perfect recipient for my word. I cast about and found this lost and longing man, a reluctant rebel, a dutiful citizen spinning in the turmoil of his unwished-for capacity to think himself into disobedience, and I thought, This one I can make my own. His longing for order (an indelible remnant, I noted with satisfaction, of the image of myself for which I had created these creatures in the first place) made his disobedience loathsome to him, and therefore something I could work with, not, as before, something that worked against my will. I would give him the opportunity to return to order, but make it difficult enough to ensure that it appeared unachievable without my assistance. I would make this one man my own, and then, given patience (and who has more patience than one with eternity on his mind?), the world would be mine once again through the man. Death and the future. I was pretty pleased with myself. Death and the future. What a canny *I am* I am, I told myself.

There he was, paralysed by conflict, and by the fleshy accident, shall we say?, of infertility that prevented its remedy; and here I was with the solution, the one and only me. Though I say it myself, I got the tone of the first calling just right.

'Abram,' I called. But he didn't respond.

'Abram,' I called again, more insistent, and he turned his head to see who was in the room.

'Abram!' I boomed this time.

'Who is it?' he whispered, not entirely surprised to be hearing a voice out of nowhere. He had been listening for me, and despairing that there would be nothing to hear. I caught him at just the right time.

'God,' I said, keeping it simple.

'Which god?'

'Your god. The Lord. I am. Forget the rest.'

He didn't answer, but let out a sigh. I kept silent for a moment, and let him taste the fear that the voice had gone. Then I gave him the word.

'Go! Leave your country, and your heritage, and your father's house, to a land I will show you. And I will make you a great nation. I will bless you and make your name a blessing. You shall be a blessing. And I will bless those who bless you, and those who damn you I will curse, and all the clans of the earth through you shall be blessed.'

And I left him to think it over.

This was new to me. Before, with the first two and then with Noah, I had spoken my curses, announced my punishment for the wrongdoings that mankind had already committed. But this time I took the initiative and I made an offer of more than a lifetime to a single man who believed that he had nothing to give me in return. In fact, he had the world to give me, the only thing in eternity that I had so far discovered I wanted. He didn't know that. He only knew that I seemed to offer something at the cost of him walking away from everything he knew, everything he had, and throwing himself and his fortunes on the mercy of a voice in his head. Take it or leave it. It was irresistible, of course. I was getting the hang of these humans. At last, I had an edge ————

———— Abram found Sarai in the kitchen, giving instructions for the following day's meals. It was the first time he had left their room in more than a week. It was also the first time that he spoke to Sarai directly since he had returned from his desert wanderings.

'Sarai, leave that. Come with me.'

She followed him out to the courtyard, where Abram sat next to her on the wall of the small fountain where Lot's children had loved to splash.

'What is it?' she asked. With the help of her bondswoman she had cleaned him up on his return from the desert, and combed the knots out of his hair, but there had been nothing they could do about the burning redness around his eyes and their haunted look as they peered at the blackness before them. They were red still, and staring, but now they were not empty. They were full of what he had to tell her. She would have been relieved to see him more animated had she not been alarmed that the gleam in his eyes was too bright, just as before they had been too dull.

'The Lord has spoken to me.'

Sarai's heart sank.

'Which lord? You have been alone for the past week,' she said wearily, brushing a fall of hair behind his ear.

'The Lord, Sarai. The Lord God.'

'The lord of the gods?'

'No, *the* Lord God. I think.'

'Just the one?'

'I heard his voice. I actually heard it. He spoke to me.'

Sarai's heart sank deeper. Despair, and now madness. The gods did not speak. Humans pleased or appeased them, and they acted on the world or didn't.

'Abram, you were dreaming.'

'No. I have been called by the Lord. Our gods, our statues can't speak to us. But this Lord called me by name. This Lord blessed me.'

'Why you? Why should this lord call you and . . . bless . . . you?'

'Because I was listening for him. Because I was waiting for a call. Because I stopped believing in our mundane gods of stone with their ordinary human relationships and their pathetic interests and rivalries. They are too much like us – more powerful, but still limited, constrained. What kind of god is constrained? Sarai, you should have heard the Lord. There is nothing this Lord cannot do. I'd been waiting for him without realising it, and Haran, if only he had not despaired, if he had waited and listened, he would have heard him, too.'

'So what did he want?'

'The Lord doesn't *want* anything. Our false little gods want sacrifice, libation, worship. But a true God has no need of anything. He only has to be heard.'

'All right, what did he say?'

'That from me will come a great nation.'

Sarai swallowed hard. The anger. The pity. Inextricable.

'Did he say how?'

'We are to go, leave this place. We must go to another land were we will begin again and build a nation.'

'And you call this not wanting anything? This land of ours is . . . where?'

'The Lord will show it to us.'

'Ah. Does it have a name?'

'He will show us the land. He promised to lead us to it.'

'Is it an empty land, or are other people already living in it?'

'It will be our land. The Lord *will* show us. Sarai, we have been offered a destiny.'

'Or destitution.'

'Destiny.'

'You may have been offered this destiny. Did your lord mention me?'

'You are my wife.'

'But he didn't say how this nation of yours will come about? How a wife who no longer menstruates will bear the beginnings of this nation of yours?'

'We must trust him. He spoke to me.'

'And so we will leave everything, the life we have made here – remade here – and start all over again. Another desert wandering. At least last time we had a destination. This time we are simply to wander aimlessly in the wilderness until your lord sees fit to find us somewhere to settle. We were young then, Abram. Perhaps our destiny is to accept our lives as they are.'

'Our future depends on trusting the Lord. I have his word.'

'But I haven't.'

'But you have mine, Sarai. You must trust me, as I will trust the Lord.'

She would have laughed out loud, but her husband's expression stopped her. He was quite mad, she realised. There were individuals in Harran who wandered the streets, fed and cared for by the townsfolk, who heard voices and spoke in riddles. It was understood that men's minds could go wrong. There was nothing to be done for them but to take care of them and let them rave and ramble their phantasms away. They were harmless, if annoying. And they spoke in the tones and wore the expression of her beloved husband as he sat in front of her explaining the future. It was always the future they spoke of, since their present was intolerable. Their eyes glowed, their minds ached towards another time, a time that did not contain the anguish of now.

Religion did not go very deep with Sarai. She went along with the rituals and the regular worship, but she was always on the periphery where it seemed that life was more a series of accidents and hard work than reward and punishment. So much had happened to her family, and as a child she had believed that the events were linked in a chain of cause and effect. Perhaps they were, but nowadays they seemed to her to be more related to the nature of the people involved. No gods were needed to account for the tragedies or even for the joys. Perhaps because she was never fully part of the ritual, because her name was never included in the incantations, she found the world itself enough to account for life. Like Abram now, all those gods milling about invisibly interfering with their lives seemed absurd to her. But unlike Abram who needed, for some reason, more than the world to explain what went wrong, Sarai was not quite led to despair by such a thought. She had gone along with religion. It did no harm and there was some comfort to be had in the idea, if not thought about too much, that we were not alone and ourselves responsible for our mistakes and follies. Still, once she was an adult, she could never persuade herself that Emtelai's and the baby's death were deserved – if she had, she would have had to revive the old fear that her childish jealousy had been punished by their extinction. This was so outrageous that it was better left unthought, or her rage at the gods who perpetrated such a crime would have been as unquenchable as Haran's. Sarai had a practical streak in her character that gave her permission to get on with life, no matter how arbitrary she suspected it might be. It was odd that Abram, so accepting and dutiful, should have come to such a passionate denial of religion. But perhaps that was the problem. Facing the reality of death and the fact of childlessness was harder for him, who believed in some higher justice, than for Sarai, who doubted its existence but did not feel obliged to confront it.

Still, even in his torment, her placid and dutiful Abram was not Haran. His loss of faith was not quite a loss of hope. He could not face such a condition. He was patient even in his despair, allowing it time to resolve his anguish with a voice inside his head. If he was mad, at least he was not dead.

The workshop was as good as finished. The woman Abram had frightened had told her story and the orders for statues had stopped coming in. Lot went every day to the shop, but there was nothing for him to do. The high priest had come to see Terah, advising him in his despair to devote himself to asking the gods for forgiveness in the hope that they would take pity on an old man and release his son from the grip of madness. Terah now spent his days at the temple, and his nights praying. It got him out of his decline. He had a purpose in life again, and the elders of Harran rallied round. His response to Abram's news of his new god was to double his sacrifice and bemoan his lot to his peers, who listened with horrified sympathy, thankful that their sons had not been so struck down.

One night Abram left his bed and smashed every remaining statue in the workshop, so there was no point in Lot even pretending that the business would pick up. There was no stock, and Lot had no talent as a chiseller and carver of images.

Abram made preparations to leave Harran for his journey to who knew where, while Sarai watched and wondered what her life would be if she stayed and ministered to the madly remorseful Terah, and what it would be if she became a nomad once again with her madly believing Abram. There was no other alternative. There was nowhere for a middle-aged woman with a father and a husband to go.

Nowhere except the same wilderness of dementia where her Abram had taken up residence. No one would have blamed her in Harran if she had stayed with Terah and let her husband vanish into his wilderness, but the prospect dismayed her. Terah was completely absorbed in the company of pious old men. Staying, she would have pottered through her later days waiting for death, and she did not have the courage to bring her life to such a foregone conclusion.

She remembered her old Abram in the desert, young and strong, her older brother, and how the life of a herdsman had suited him. He had a way with animals and he had learned to tend them. When they had trekked away from Ur to escape disgrace and tragedy, Abram had blossomed with his animals. He loved the journeys in the half-light, the cool black night sky smeared with stars, and the sweltering days lazing inside the tent, protected from the blazing sun. He had been strong and fit then, Sarai recalled, striding between the encampment and his herds like the master of the universe. She remembered the lambs and kids whose births they had attended, and the pleasure and astonishment at being present at the beginning of new life, and his fierce determination to keep sick animals alive, refusing to sleep and nursing them back to health, or weeping tears of loss if they succumbed. He was fully alive in that moving landscape, striding with the dust in his hair and sand on his eyelashes. He was her Abram. She remembered him, and how she had loved him. She missed him – missed them both – terribly. Old now, it was easy to forget the pain that had begun for her on their betrothal and left her alone all those nights in the desert when the brother could not make himself a husband.

Perhaps, after all, there was some sense in Abram's plan to leave Harran. Though his new god was his excuse, he had the same memories as Sarai: did he feel a return to that life would soothe his mental agony? Whatever his intentions, the effect might be the same. And what was there to keep them now in Harran? As Sarai thought of it, she wondered if the return of the dutiful, plodding Abram of their life in Harran was what she, herself, wanted. Her recollections of their youth in the wilderness did not make such a return to normality attractive. She found, in spite of her alarm for Abram's state of mind and a fear of yet again walking away from their settled life, a kind of excitement building in her, borne perhaps of nostalgia. But it brought a sense of possibility, of movement through the world, of change that she hadn't known until then that she had been missing. The nomadic life might clear Abram's mind of the despair that caused voices in his head. And even if it did not, she thought, Abram could have his god, and she, perhaps, could have something of the old Abram, and room, as well, to breathe.

His decision to leave had already improved his state of mind. There was no more talk of the lord, only plans for disengaging themselves from the city, what they needed to take with them, which servants could be persuaded to come, who would stay and look after Terah. He was full of energy.

Not long before they left, Lot came to Sarai.

'Can we come with you?' he asked nervously.

'We don't know where we are going, and Abram isn't well,' she said. 'If you stay, you will be head of the household. You can rebuild the business and be your own master.'

As she spoke, she realised that it was just this prospect that alarmed Lot. He could not imagine himself in charge of a family, making the decisions. He wanted to tag along, even if his leader had no idea where he was going, he wanted to follow. Even if Abram was mad as a rabid bat, it was better to go with him than be in charge of his own life.

'But *you* are going. You're sensible. I trust you.'

She thanked Lot for his faith in her. Why not take Lot with them? He was a willing worker, if told what to do. Another man, and one not likely to get carried away with godly thoughts, would be useful. And she was fond of the girls. She would have missed them. Terah would be well taken care of by the remaining servants and his new old cronies.

Terah did not bat an eyelid when Sarai told him that they were to leave. He sat in his shaded corner of the courtyard and nodded solemnly.

'Yes, that would be for the best,' he said. 'The gods will appreciate Abram paying such a penance, and it's right that you should go with him. You are his wife.' A shadow passed across his face as if he had just remembered something, but it passed like a wind-chased cloud. Sarai let Terah's misunderstanding of Abram's motives go. He didn't mention Lot, but she didn't get the feeling that he would be greatly missed. Terah was settling in well to the life of an elder, and learning to wear his suffering as a badge of pride among

them. Perhaps the rest of the family had become an embarrassment to him. He had found a life for himself, and he was
glad to see the back of them.

FAMINE

Now the Lord had said unto Abram, Get thee out of thy country, and from thy kindred, and from thy father's house, unto a land that I will show thee: And I will make of thee a great nation, and I will bless thee, and make thy name great; and thou shalt be a blessing: And I will bless them that bless thee, and curse him that curseth thee; and in thee shall all families of the earth be blessed.

GENESIS 12:1–3

Again.

For the second time in their lives Abram and Sarai relinquished the past. Once again they left everything, but this time they were truly wanderers. They had no destination, apart from a vague promise locked inside Abram's head, that there would, sometime, somewhere, be one. *To a land that I will show you.* That was where they were going, according to Abram. He gathered the small party together on the outskirts of Harran: Lot, his wife, their three girls, their children, the dozen servants who agreed to go along, and told them, his eyes burning with the glory of it, 'We will be shown our new land.' His conviction had to do for all of them. A second-hand assurance of destination did not sound promising to anyone, and yet, in spite of doubting that they were going anywhere much at all, they went along. Lot and his family, because life had become too difficult in Harran; the servants perhaps for the adventure, perhaps out of a fondness for Abram and Sarai; and Sarai, because she wanted what was no longer in Harran and knew no other way to find it. She was lost already, she had come to the end of the life she had lived before then; her safety in this world in the form of love had vanished. Her heart had closed and locked. What did she have to fear from the wilderness? At least she would be lost and moving. In Harran there was only stagnation.

There was another difference between that first trek from Ur and now; then they had taken all their wealth with them, now they had very little that was surplus to their needs. Abram bought the sheep and goats, this time not in order to appear to be an ordinary nomadic group but for subsistence. Abram took only what he had to from Harran to get started on their new journey. They bought sheep and goats and donkeys, they bought tents. They were truly wanderers in the desert.

'We will be provided for,' Abram said calmly.

Sarai envied his conviction, but she felt no very great alarm at leaving most of their worldly goods behind. She was almost intrigued and energised by the new uncertainty of her life, and after all, their former wealth had not provided her with any great security. Any life was better than the sadness of those last weeks in Harran. And when she saw Abram in the middle of the new herds, surveying and checking the animals, and watched the twisted ropes of muscle in his neck visibly relax, and the throb in his troubled temples ease as he bent to examine a pregnant ewe, she believed that whatever the future held, there would, on the way to it, be some peace of mind. There would be some sense in rising in the morning, because even if they didn't know where they were going, they knew that the animals depended on them for pasture and water. There was something to care for. They would move from well to well, from town to town, from desert encampment to encampment with no less reason than any other travelling group who did not have the personal word of an invisible lord to justify their existence. They would buy and sell and barter according to their needs. They had no settled place, nor any destination, but they would have a rhythm of necessity to their lives. There was life to think about beyond their own, and Sarai hoped the anguish that had caused the voice inside Abram's head would ease and leave them both in peace.

Yes, of course, she saw what she looked for. She ached for life to return to the way it once had been. She wanted the rhythm of their old nomadic life, or the throb of the time when they were first lovers to wash away the memory of her anger, the taste of bitterness, her unsought vision of life as arid and wasted. She wanted love back so that she would not have to consider what a life without love might mean. That was why she willingly left her sedentary life; that was why she let it happen ————————

———————— Ha! *She* let it happen! What had she done but follow orders I had given my chosen one? I spoke and Abram obeyed. *That* is what happened. That is how it happened. She may talk of madness and despair, and of voices caused by anguish. But the voice was mine, the plan was

mine. The relation was between Abram and *I am*. I had
made an us of him and me far more compelling than she
could imagine with her time-tainted human love, which
had produced nothing. Between Abram and me, a future
would be created. I could give him what she had failed to
provide. She was just flesh and bone. I was almighty, I was
eternal. She speaks of sheep and goats. I had destiny in my
gift. Abram was mine ————

———— Yes, it may be. This was a time of raw sentiment for Sarai, of a final clinging to hope. It was the
recollection of a spark, a brief moment of foolish reaching
for what had gone. She had faced hopelessness and for a
short period she grasped at the past, and the illusion that it
was retrievable.

And she loved those first months in the desert. Perhaps she
knew all along that there could be no return, that life was lived
in only one direction and memory merely tormented the dis-
contented with its capacity to look backwards, but, as in a
dream where the dreamer suspects they might be dreaming
but refuses to vacate the dreamscape, Sarai allowed memory to
whisper to her of the past and chose to believe it said future.
Though she thought she was humouring her deluded husband
by going along on his trek to nowhere as ordered by no one,
she was in truth no more in touch with reality than Abram.
Foolish old woman. She heard no inner voice of salvation, but
in her own way she was just as capable of self-deception.

Abram's *voice* had been silent since it told him to leave,

but he did not doubt that he was following its purpose and that it was following his progress. Love *was* recovered on that journey, but it was not Abram's old love for Sarai. He was kind and gentle, and treated her with consideration and respect as was due a wife of decades, but when they made camp, he erected a tent for Sarai beside his own. Now she slept apart from Abram for the first time since they had married. She would have been a foolish woman indeed to expect either of them to feel the same physical passion for each other after all this time, but they had retained their physical love until this crisis; it was no longer discovery, it had become history, and they had touched each other with the memory of all the years between them, with the eroticism of time. They had touched and been touched by their familiarity with every part of each other and delighted by revisiting and remembering. Even now, Abram had not lost his passion, his capacity for devotion, but it was focused away from Sarai, turned simultaneously inwards and towards eternity, missing his flesh and blood wife entirely. He loved her, of course, dutifully, as one loves a long-standing partner in life, but he desired the one who promised what she had failed to achieve. Sarai saw him, at night, wandering from his tent, in the light of the stars, absorbed and utterly abstracted, waiting. The look on his face reminded her of all those years ago when Terah had spoken to him of marriage and she caught him glancing at her in an entirely new way, seeing her afresh. Now that look was for what lay beyond the massed stars and the uncountable sands of the desert. The world itself was his promised bride, and he had no doubt that the secrets it held would be revealed to him. Could Sarai be jealous of the world? Could she envy a phantom voice that distracted her Abram into another love? Oh, yes. Yes. Sometimes, of course, in the midst of her solitary raging, she would realise how ridiculous her anger was against a spectral voice engendered by despair. And then her rage would double, because her jealousy was not just ridiculous, but impotent against a seduction by a dream. A real rival would have been preferable. At least, had Abram taken a concubine rather than this lord of his, she would have retained her position as senior wife. Now, as he mooned over his phantasm, she became entirely irrelevant.

They journeyed south and east, according to Abram's instinct. It didn't matter to Sarai which direction they took. There was plenty to keep her busy. She was in charge of the smooth running of the group, much as she had been during their sedentary life in Harran, supervising their food supplies, helping to spin and make cloth to replace the wind- and sand-blown garments as they wore away. The girls and the children would come to her with their arguments, and their complaints against their mothers, just as their mothers would sit with Sarai and bemoan the lives they were leading and the depleting effects of pregnancy and child-care. The servants brought her their problems. And Abram brought her sick and abandoned kids and lambs to nurse back to health. She had a way with sick animals, he said. She soothed and sorted. Nothing in any of their difficulties seemed overwhelming to her, it was easy enough to cut through the tensions, to murmur easing words and find quite obvious solutions. Only her own existence seemed insoluble, and yet it went on day by day. She had a function and she had everyone's trust and respect. She liked the practicality of life on the move. No one guessed that she was in any pain. Her pain, like Abram's, was about what could not be touched or seen.

It isn't even true to say that Abram did not love her any more. He did. But she was no longer the central passion of his life. He did not sink into her arms at night as if that was the final purpose of the day's doings. He did not tell her how he desired her and how he needed her, either with his voice or his body. And worst of all, in failing to do these things, he did not tell her how much she needed him. It may be that this was the most painful loss, the one she could least of all face: she no longer needed Abram. She was cut adrift in a world in which she was able to manage perfectly well, but from which all purpose had been abolished. She could have imagined, though she dared not do it, an existence without Abram, a life of her own if Abram should leave or die. This was the most fearful thing. Abram was no longer the object of her life, the source of her being. If, after a lifetime, she no longer needed Abram, what had that lifetime been for?

Whatever the answer, it had certainly not been for the purpose of reproduction. She might nurture Abram's sick lambs and her nieces, but it had not been given to her to bring children into the world and grow them into the next generation. Whether her body was at fault, or Abram's capacity to engender children, or even if it was the will of the gods or Abram's lord, it was a fact. Perhaps there were other women in the same circumstances, but she did not

know them. In any case, it was her life, her body that was
definitively deprived; the lack was the centre of her life as
she looked back on it then. Whatever might have been,
was not, because she had failed to have children. And what
was, their aimless wandering in the desert, their loss of
home and birthright, was the result of the same failure.
Childlessness was as close to Sarai as her heartbeat or her
guilt over Emtelai and the baby, and now closer both to
Abram and Sarai than they were to each other. This also
was the way of the world, but no one had thought to
mention it.

They came to a land called Canaan. It was no different from
the other places they had travelled through, a mixed land of
desert and wells, lush enough in parts to sustain herds, with
settlements here and there but with nothing of the urban
sophistication of Ur or even of Harran. It was distinguished
from the lands around by being the homeland of the
Canaanite people, descendants it was said of Ham, who had
so disgraced himself with his drunken father, Noah, and
who was the brother of their ancestor Shem. The Canaanites
worshipped gods very similar to those they had left behind in
Harran, and lived in settlements or travelling bands like
themselves. They took no offence at Abram's group moving
through and making camp in their land. There was room
enough for all of them. It seemed to Sarai to be just another
place they were passing through on their journey of promised but never-to-be-reached destination. But she was
wrong, at least in part.

They made camp just outside the village of Shechem, not

far from a glade of oak trees called Moreh, which was the sacred place of the local deity to whom the people there-abouts sacrificed and prayed for the well-being of their herds and crops. One morning, not long after they arrived, Abram entered Sarai's tent in the yellow light of the early hours. Even in the dimness of dawn his face glowed with excitement.

'We have arrived,' he told her, kneeling beside her bed. 'This is our destination.'

She turned his words over in her sleepy mind until they made Abram's kind of sense.

'Here? This place is where we were coming to all along? Shechem?'

It seemed a long way to come for nothing very special.

'This land. Canaan. This is where my seed will develop into a nation.'

She stopped herself from snapping that so far his seed had failed to develop into a single baby, and she could not see how it was going to make the leap directly into nationhood now. Abram never was strong on irony and he looked even less likely to appreciate it at the moment.

'Won't the Canaanites have something to say about it?' she could not resist saying.

'Sarai,' he said, whispering urgently, trying to focus her mind on the importance of what he was saying, 'I have seen the Lord. He appeared to me last night, and told me that this was to become our land. It is his promise to us.'

'To you,' Sarai insisted. 'What did he look like?'

She treated her husband's fantasies as she would a child who mistook its dream for reality.

'I saw him. Yes, I saw him, but what I saw can't be described. I was walking in the glade of trees, and he was there, in front of me, but though my eyes saw him, he was a presence more than a figure, an air, a quality of light. There are no words, no picture that I could make of him.'

'Him?'

'Of course.'

Of course. That much of this unpicturable vision would have been blindingly obvious. Of course.

'And he said?'

'I give this land to your seed.'

'That's all?'

'Yes.'

'He didn't say how?'

'Sarai, you don't understand. This is the Lord. He has revealed this place to me and what it is to become. Believe me, he is not like any other god we have ever known. If you had heard him, seen him . . .'

'But I haven't.'

'But if you had, you would understand. This Lord is all powerful. He can do anything. He is the Lord of the mountain peak who sits above all things and beings, all other gods, all men, higher than any, more potent than any. The world is in his gift. The Lord, this Lord High God, has chosen me. He has chosen us. We are to be his people.'

'What do you have to do to transform your seed into a nation?'

'Only to believe the Lord. That is all. He requires nothing else.'

'Not yet, he doesn't. So the Canaanites will just bow

before you and go off to find some other place to live, will they? And you will proceed to start a nation. With whom will you do this, Abram?'

'Sarai, the Lord will provide.'

'How are you supposed to claim this place for yourself and your mountainous lord?'

'We will travel through the land and build altars to him, proclaim him as the Lord of this country and of our people.'

So it seemed that Shechem was not to be their final stopping place. Now they were to become the entourage of a peripatetic teacher with the word of a new lord in his ear, wandering and proclaiming. Life, Sarai decided, takes the most unexpected turns.

Abram built an altar to his lord in the sacred place of the local Shechemite god at Moreh. The local people didn't seem to mind at all. The more gods the merrier as far as they were concerned. People stopped and listened politely as Abram proclaimed his new god, and although they were unconvinced at his claims of the superiority of this lord over the other deities, they accepted that to Abram, his personal god was better than the rest. Everyone felt the same. Some gods you worshipped, but your own god held a special place in your heart. It amused them, Sarai thought, to see Abram so passionate about his. Religion was what made the world work, there was no reason to limit the possibilities and every reason to add to the pantheon of gods another who might come in useful. These were practical believers, as the family of Shem once had been, until the strange passion of Haran had tainted them with special longings.

They pulled up their stakes and continued south into the hill country between Bethel and Ai, and there too Abram added an altar of his lord to the local holy place. And so they went: Abram built altars and proclaimed, and the rest of them got on with life on the move and became quite used to it. They had a holy man among them now. Abram, Sarai's brother and husband, seemed lost. The reliable, stable presence of his uncle, more like a father, was gone from Lot's life. To all intents and purposes Sarai ran the little group, while Abram walked beneath the sun and stars, pacing the days and nights away with glazed eyes, intent upon doing the work of his lord, while the rest of them followed in his footsteps and kept a reasonably sensible life going. Lot was distressed. He was quite unable to understand what had happened to Abram. He had no interest in this new god or any other: he wanted life simple. Sarai tried to reassure him, and he came to her now instead of Abram when he was confused or troubled. And all this time, she suppressed the fury and disappointment, and smoothed the surface of the turmoil in which she was living. Was her Abram mad? Were they following the wayward steps of a man who had lost his reason? Sarai had no doubt that they were. And yet a kind of normality emerged, a sort of ordinariness that they all hankered after. It did not look much like the normality they had once known as a settled, wealthy family, but the days and nights of wandering became their days and nights, and Abram's impassioned daydream led them through the land as well as any group. Abram was inspired, but it was easy enough to ignore that and to feel they were just another band of travellers making a living in a difficult world. There is nothing so extraordinary in the universe that humanity can't make mundane and everyday ————

———— I, who belonged to eternity with no beginning and no end, who had created the earth and the seas, the day and the night, mountains, valleys, rivers, the frozen waste, the searing desert, the seed, the egg, the male, the female, and seething, sentient life to flourish on my world; I, who am *I am*, the Word, the Creator, the Destroyer, beyond all life and death; I, the omnipotent, the omniscient, the singular, discovered at last what it was to be the object of love.

It came as a surprise to me. I had not built this into creation. Why would I even have thought of it? My universe was a perfect machine for self-replication, a divinely ordained mechanism that ensured decay and renewal at every level from the cell to the cosmos. All life, from the single cell to the myriad-celled collective that called itself an individual, had a built-in necessity to reproduce, to make a living and to degrade back into the substance of the earth from which it was made. It was simple and self-ordering. I began it, and it continued because it had no other choice but to be the way I made it. There was no need for a special relationship of feeling between one individual and another. I had not created it, had not even conceived of it, because it was simply not necessary for the mechanism to work. And yet, that is what happened, without my will, without my consent, as a kind of accidental by-product of the gift of self-consciousness. Of course, I need not have given them self-consciousness, the pattern of the universe did not require it, but I made humankind in my own image, they were to be my mirror. And they made something of their own, and discovered that their self-consciousness implied the separate existence of the other that I could never had imagined in my eternal solitude. An independent awareness like a polished glass which one conscious being could peer into and see itself reflected, and reflect back from its own consciousness to the other. This reflective process they call *us* and *love*. I had been the creator, the punisher, but I had never been part of an *us*. How could I when I was eternally, unalterably, *I am*? And yet now I myself experienced this strange capacity that humanity had developed in spite of me. It turned towards me and I felt, for the first time in all time itself, the power of something I had had no hand in creating. Abram, given the promise of a dream come true, had turned his human feelings towards me. He loved me. Abram was mine in a way that no other creature on earth had been mine before. My mirror mirrored me at last and showed me what I had never dreamed of.

Adam and Eve and their offspring had learned to fear me. This was right. It was as I expected. Noah had been dumbly obedient, and then, perhaps noticing that he had done nothing to help any but his own flesh and blood, spent the rest of his time in an alcoholic miasma. That was the limit of my relations to the creatures I had made. I made rules for them, and they learned to obey or suffered the consequences. But it had not resulted in a humanity that pleased me. With

Abram my approach was different. I instructed him only to leave the security of his life and trust in me. I looked for a man with an overwhelming need and I made him a promise, I did not issue any threat or prohibition. And the remarkable result was not just obedience but devotion. I asked only that he trust me – though why he should have done, for the life of me I cannot say. I had discovered something deeply and specifically human: the wish to trust, to love. I had only to ask it of someone whose hunger for it was great, and it was mine. And I had not even known it was there.

Always, always, I had to learn from the life I had made. This love that Abram turned on me, like a beam from my own sun on the darkness of dawn, was beyond the power even of *I am* to imagine. It was the greatest surprise I had ever had ————

———— Yet love was no surprise to Sarai. She had grown with love, was placed inside its cocoon with her first breath of air. She suckled it from the milky breast, felt it in the heartbeat inside the body that held her in its arms. Love grasped at her before words formed in her mind, before fear and friendship developed. Love came to her in every breath she took as if those to whom she belonged had exhaled it into the air. It was the very source of life. Love, indeed, might even have been implicated in death. And all the difficulty she had known could also be placed at love's door. Love was so obvious, so soon, that when it took its leave of her, she had no way of understanding her existence in the world. The heartbeat stopped, the air was no longer breathable, and she lost her place in the universe. Love surprised *her* only by its absence.

Yes, she managed their new life well enough, but whether she was living in it is another matter entirely. Perhaps, if she had known more of the world, if she had been born many, many generations later when the world whispered its centuries of experience to those who would listen, she might have been grateful to have possessed so much love for so long and reckoned herself lucky that she had had any at all. But I doubt it. Love wraps you in its embrace, but it does not prepare you for its loss. The shock is not that you are no longer loved by your beloved, nor that you no longer love, but that love *can* be lost. The death of love filled Sarai with a retrospective terror that love was never what she thought it had been; hers or Abram's; that she might have been deceived all her life about the central fact of her existence. The love she had known, when she had known it, was indestructible, an absolute truth. Now that the absolute truth had dissolved, it could not have been either absolute or truth. What had it been all along? She had thought that whatever happened in the rest of the world – the tragedy of Haran, the death of Emtelai, even her lurking guilt and fear that she was not completely part of the family – the love between Abram and her was unbreachable. It was more real to Sarai than tragedy, death and guilt. It was the very nature of her world, the bedrock. And now it had changed and shown itself to be mere *feeling*. An accidental convergence of feeling. A random event that circumstances could alter. A mutual comfort that was subsumed by a greater need that had not been satisfied by their time together. Love needed more than itself to survive. In the end we are nothing more than the machinery of the universe, and love merely an element in its mechanism. Only reproduction mattered: to the universe and to humans. And when it failed in individual cases, it mattered not at all to the universe. Only the individual cases cared, driven as they were to do the bidding of necessity and finding themselves purposeless. Lot had not had the fortune of a wall of love as Sarai had and she had pitied him for that, yet Lot's children served the purpose of the world as well as hers would have. And she, the recipient of love, was left with only her own life, her time not yet over.

You could say that Abram was more attuned to the universe than Sarai. He raged against the futility, and found in his desperation another way to retrieve love and promise, whereas Sarai discovered the truth of the world, the coldness of the universe, the callousness of whatever was responsible for the treadmill of continuation. Love was a lost dream, and life itself shrivelled.

Now there was famine in the land – as if the world itself were concurring with Sarai's view of it. This was not Mesopotamia, where sophisticated cities took precautions against such things. The Canaanites had no stores of grain against drought and crop failure. The pastures dried up as Abram's entourage reached the Negev, and scarcity was everywhere. The land of Canaan became as barren and emptied of promise as Sarai herself.

'We must go into Egypt,' Abram decided.

It seemed they had to make their own way in life just like regular folk who lacked the blessings of Abram's lord. Sarai was tired of this game.

'And what does your lord have to say about this, about leaving this land he promised to your seed, which we've traipsed across, building altars and sacrificing our finest animals to him? What of that great nation he mentioned, and all the blessings we were going to receive? This land, which we've given up everything, home, family, security, to get to, cannot sustain even our handful of sheep let alone our promised posterity. Perhaps you could have a word with him. Or has he offered us Egypt instead? I dare say the Pharaoh will be delighted to hand it over to us.'

Abram's face darkened. 'This is a test of faith,' he said, with the coldest look in his eyes she had ever seen, and he went away without another word. She had failed the test. This new icy Abram made that clear as they prepared to leave. Sarai knew how he hated her ever-sharpening tongue, her acid disbelief, but it was all she had to sustain her in the chaos of her life. He thought it easy to deride his faith, but he did not know how she envied him his lord, or rather his passionate vision and his belief in it. How much simpler it would have been if this lord had spoken to her too, and she had been compelled to believe that life had some point. She might have pretended. Then Abram would have embraced her and they would have been united in love and purpose once more. But her lack of faith in Abram's vision, her exclusion from it, had degraded *her* love. The truth was she did not love Abram well enough any more to sacrifice her scepticism to him. That was the centre of her agony.

They left the land of starvation and went down into Egypt. Abram did not speak to Sarai again during that journey until they were at the limit of the Negev. It was clear, however, that he had been thinking about her. Often, she would look up, as if someone had called her name, and see Abram, pausing from whatever task he was engaged in, looking back at her. It was not unlike all those decades before when she caught him glancing at her with a new aspect in his eyes, seeing her as a woman when before she had been a sister. Now, his look was sharp and analytical, and she remembered, too, how in his workshop he had stared and stared at an unworked piece of wood or stone to find its real nature from which he would carve the statue that existed within it. There had been more warmth in his regard for the inert stone or wood than she saw now as he examined her from a distance.

It may have been his first realisation that the love had soured between them. Sarai had been struggling with this knowledge ever since those last weeks in Harran, seeing in his devotion to his new lord the disappearance of their love, but Abram had not thought about it in that way. Absorbed as he was in his new passion, he had not given Sarai any thought at all. He did not know that he had transferred his love, the meaning of his life from *us* to a vision in his own head. Now, it seemed to dawn on him, or at least he appeared to be looking at Sarai and wondering who she was, what she was to him after all, having known her all her life. Sarai saw in his glance the sudden recognition of the distance she had travelled from the chamber of his heart to existing simply as another object in the external world. An infinite, unimaginable distance not so very many months before; now, between the two of them, in the Negev, at the brink of Egypt, it was an accomplished fact. She had known it already in her own dismayed heart, but it took that new look in Abram's eyes to establish it finally as a reality as they travelled south into Egypt, away from their promised land to the land of plenty.

He came to Sarai in her tent one night, waking her from a fitful dream.

'You are still a good-looking woman,' he said.

So strange. Her husband, her lover for all that time past, speaking these words with calculating eyes, and in a voice that might have been describing the terrain they were to pass through.

'It could be dangerous for me if the Egyptians think you are my wife. We are strangers here, we don't know what kind of men these are. I have heard that they appreciate older women. They might kill me on your account. We mustn't provoke them. It will go better for us if we tell them that you're my sister.'

It will go better for us. Sarai absorbed his words in her abdomen, not through her ears or brain. There were so many thoughts caught in his words that she could only feel them, not unravel their meaning with her mind.

'A sister again,' she breathed.

She had not been Abram's sister since she had become his child bride.

'In Egypt. It's purely practical.'

And still, it seemed, the anxious child in her had not been erased by the years of their love: she actually gained a little relief in retaining that much relationship with her husband and family. He had not said half-sister, he had not said that she was nothing to the house of Shem. Even that degree of belonging was better than none, she thought, beneath her horror at Abram's words. The fearful child who craved connection desperately sought and found that much comfort. At the same time, a middle-aged woman looked at her husband of decades as he repudiated her, and saw the infinity of troubled distance that lay between men and women in the world.

'How fortunate,' she murmured. 'We won't even have to lie.'

Her brother did not reply, but left her tent to get some rest before they began their sojourn in Egypt.

He was right. She was still an attractive woman, at least in Egyptian eyes. Word got around that a group of Habiru had arrived to escape the famine in Canaan and that their leader had a handsome sister. The Pharaoh was known to take an interest in foreign women, and it was not long before they received a visit from his emissary welcoming them to Egypt and inviting Sarai to the palace. The request, with a good deal of flourish and fine words, was made, of course, to Abram, while Sarai sat beside him in the tent, receiving not a glance or a nod from the ambassador.

'My master requests the company of your sister this evening.'

As he spoke, slaves arrived with gifts sent by the Pharaoh, evidence of his generosity and goodwill to the Habiru whose future existence, it was clear to both parties, now depended on his benevolence. Their camp filled with the Pharaoh's largesse: sheep, cattle and camels, male and female slaves, donkeys and she-asses; enough to ensure a comfortable living for the small group all the rest of their days. A king's ransom, you might say. Did Sarai see a shadow cross Abram's face before he took refuge in the formality that was so useful in enabling transactions of this kind to be made without overt disgrace to either party? She was sure it was so, and he did not look her in the eyes as he nodded his permission to the Pharaoh's ambassador to take her to his master.

Great fear will provoke the craven stranger to emerge in the best of men. Perhaps not the very best of men, but such paragons had not been born in Sarai's time. Abram's fear of death at the hand of a sexually covetous Egyptian ruler was not simply about his immediate survival, but a greater fear, beyond his physical safety, of the death of promise. His extinction without issue would have denied what was now the centre of his life – it would have contradicted the word of his lord, and made a nonsense of the faith that he had discovered in his terror of futility. Sarai was sure this was so. She made herself sure of it as she accompanied the ambassador to his master's quarters in the royal palace. How else could she have suppressed the implied futility of her own existence? ————

———— They are never to be trusted. None of them. Deceivers of me, of each other, of themselves, how can anyone who is not me plumb the depths of their deviousness when they themselves don't comprehend its amplitude and complexity? For the first time I found myself wishing I had the human capacity to deny. I, too, have my yearnings; I, too, would defend myself against too much disappointment if I could. This all-seeing business has its drawbacks. The peace of my eternity had been desecrated by mistrust and anxiety – new-found consequences of my tinkering with infinite emptiness, of my creation of the other.

Even he, even Abram, who first recognised and proclaimed me, could not suppress a wily and wilful human nature. Naturally, like all humanity, he could delude himself about his true motives, but I was not blessed with the capacity to overlook what it was inconvenient for me to see. Who was there to bless me with such a gift? I saw what I saw, and that was everything. I who had created the tree of the knowledge of good and evil, how could I choose not to know what there was to be known? Abram loved me, he believed in me, he had faith in my word, trusted that my promise to him would be fulfilled, and yet in spite of his wish to be mine, in spite of his being mine, there was a place of uncertainty, a dark spot where the possibility of his being wrong survived in spite of his desperate need. A seed from the forbidden fruit of the knowledge of good and evil had stuck in humanity's gullet and forever raised its doubts.

She thought only that Abram betrayed her when he presented her on a plate to Pharaoh. But it was more profound than that. To betray his human love was one thing, but to betray his trust in me, in *I am*, who had chosen him out of all the world and all of time, that was betrayal indeed. She and I, though rivals for the affection of our chosen one, were more allied than she knew, or would admit to knowing. What, after all, could it mean that Abram had relinquished to the seed of another man, the woman, the sister-wife through whom my promise of his posterity, the

nationhood of the Habiru, had to come? What sort of obedience was that? What kind of faith? What love?

When I told Noah to build an ark, he built an ark, he did
not hedge his bets. Wasn't that what Abram was doing? How
could there be danger in Egypt when I had promised him
success? What could there possibly be to fear with my protection? But I saw something worse than a less than perfect
faith: I saw resistance, the old wilfulness, the desire to control
his own destiny. Did he think I would not know what he was
doing, giving Sarai to another man? Did he dare to issue me
with a challenge? Yes, he did. If his faith was incomplete, so
was his fear. This puny creature of my invention, without
even a child to his name, demanded proof of my intentions,
and threatened to throw his posterity in my face. And what
could I do? Could I kill him? Could I turn my back on him?
I had my needs, now, too. Drawn out of me by the feeble,
fleshy creatures I had made one idle moment in eternity. I,
the creator, had not created love: the creatures I made in my
own image had done that, invented alliance and turned it into
desire, longing, need, yes, love. And now I loved, as if I had
caught it like a virus, as if I were their creation, as if I were a
mere emotional being like them. I who drifted with eternity,
solitary, needing nothing, I, it seemed, had fallen – oh, how
appropriate the metaphor – in love. How could I kill Abram?
Abram was all I had ─────────

───────── It is astonishing how the breath continues
and the heart pumps. Believe in mechanism. Nothing else

endures. Mechanism alone is impervious to the emptiness of the universe, to the sterility of its own purpose. Only mechanism persists beyond hope and reason. There was not much of a notion of natural science then, but Sarai observed her continuing intake of breath, her throbbing heart, and knew that there resided the power and mystery of existence. All any of us have in reality is the heart beating, the breath coming and going; life ticking on with no concern for love or heartache, for hope or emptiness. Whatever Abram's lord might have been, for Sarai only mechanism could master her despair. Where nothing else exists, nothing else makes sense.

That night in Pharaoh's house Sarai experienced leaving home in a way she had not when she left Ur and then her father in Harran. For the first time, she was a stranger in a strange land. Her place all her life had been with Abram, as brother, as husband, as homeland; no landscape was strange while Abram accompanied her through it. Nothing new, no change struck ice into her heart, because she remained where she belonged. She was fortunate to have had it for so long, I suppose. And yet, it seems that love and security do not accumulate. Many years of safety and certainty of love disappeared that night into cold reality as if they had never existed. They provided no protection, left no residue of strength with which she could sustain herself in this first moment of utter aloneness and desolation.

The Pharaoh was an elderly man, but his hands were soft and supple as the finest gloves made from the silky underbelly of day-old kid. No chisel had ever slipped and scored the skin, no rough, raw material had sanded his fingertips until they grew protective pads of leather and lost their sensitivity.

Nothing had ever been worked by those fingers other than
the sheerest silks and cotton, and the choicest flesh. Those
remarkable hands parted the robe his servants had wrapped
around Sarai after bathing and scenting her, and set about
their investigation of her body with such delicacy that they
might have been the antennae of a butterfly. His fingertips
barely grazed her breasts, her belly and her thighs, needing
only the most minute stimulation to awaken his desire. His
face, and his body once he had shed his own light robe, was
hairless and smooth as an infant. There was no coarse beard,
no dark curling growth on his limbs and chest to disturb the
perfect contact between his flesh and hers. He smelt of
spiced orange, his lips, sipping at her moist skin in the heat-
still night, travelling the length of her body, felt cool and
fresh. Her Abram had been an ardent lover, but this man was
an artist who had distilled vast experience into a masterclass
on love. He seemed with the lightest touch of his tongue
tasting the salt of her tears to be savouring the precise quality of her dismay, and testing it, like an alchemist, with his
fingers reaching between her thighs, against the rise of her
desire which, oblivious to her heartache and in spite of her
tears, began to flutter into life under his expert touch and
gentle murmurings. She was not crying for Abram. She had
been deserted by him. She was weeping for her own abandonment, for the newness, and even the sweetness of the
hands on her body, for the unfamiliar voice that murmured
sensual sounds in her ear, for all her fears of being cast out
and sent away now come true. She was alone, left to drift in
the tide for the first time in her life. This was a gentle,
cradling tide. This practised, pleasure-loving-and-giving

Pharaoh treated Sarai like an exotic treasure and showed her possibilities of physical love she hadn't dreamed of, but the universe was too large, too empty and she was too alone in it all of a sudden for her to appreciate that she might have been given up by Abram to be raped by someone far worse.

When he pushed her thighs apart and prepared to enter her, he whispered, 'I will commend your brother to the gods for giving you to me.'

Sarai spoke for the first time as she felt the pressure against her vulva, which had received no other man than Abram. 'It was my husband who gave me to you.'

She was speaking to herself, telling herself the truth of what was happening to her.

'I was not told of any husband. I heard only of your brother, Abram,' the Pharaoh said, surprised at his poor information. The pressure against her vulva remained but was stilled.

'Abram is my husband. He lied. He feared you would have him killed if you thought he stood in your way.'

The pressure withered. The Pharaoh sat up.

'Is it true? He is your husband? He thought that I would kill a man to take his wife?'

There was a silence as he looked into Sarai's face and saw she was speaking the truth. Then a look of distaste came over his fine chiselled features.

'What kind of people are you that expect such barbarous behaviour? Is this how you treat each other? To kill a man merely for a woman?' He paused, feeling his ardour fade to nothing at the thought. 'It is out of the question. I cannot make love to you.'

Sarai decided not to take it personally. He got up and put his robe back on, then handed her the robe that had been discarded on the floor beneath his. With great delicacy, proving himself the gentleman he was, he turned his back as she covered herself. He was quivering with offended pride as he spun round and indicated with a regal sweep of his hand that she take her place on a couch. For a while he paced up and down in front of Sarai, stopping once or twice absent-mindedly to fill her wine goblet and offer her delicacies from a tray.

'Do the men of the Habiru kill each other over women?' he asked eventually.

'No, my lord, not as a rule. But we are strangers here. People tell stories about foreign places. You hear things. It was said . . . My husband could not be sure what kind of reception he would have. It was a precaution.'

It was clear enough that the Egyptians did not kill each other over women, but Sarai was not certain that a blow to their pride would not merit the death penalty. Even so, she heard herself excusing Abram to the morally outraged Pharaoh with a certain amount of wonder. She recalled the sweet gentleness of his hands exploring her body, and a part of her wanted to rest her head against his breast and howl her misery at him. Instead, she tried to assuage his anger against her husband for a crime that appalled both of them.

The Pharaoh paced and brooded for some time. Then he sat on a chair opposite Sarai. 'My dear,' he said, in paternal tones, 'you and I have been used disgracefully. Shall I have him put to death? You are welcome to take your place among my concubines in the palace. You will be well looked after, and, who knows, in time, I might overcome my . . . physical distaste at your revelation.'

'Please, my lord, let him live. There are people who depend on him. And he has been under great mental pressure. Let us leave your country in peace, and perhaps he will have learned something about strangers.'

Sarai stayed the rest of the night in the palace with the Pharaoh who, now he could no longer feel sexual desire for her, became a charming and informative host. She heard about Egyptian society and the nature of monarchy, and in turn she told him about the peoples of the desert, about the life of wandering tribes, and about the life of women, her life – though she omitted to mention her other relation to Abram, telling him she had been adopted as an orphan by Terah, since she feared such a revelation might be too much for her host. She did not know that brothers and sisters regularly produced heirs to the Egyptian throne. At last, late into the night, they slept, chastely, in separate rooms, and in the morning the Pharaoh's servant woke Sarai and took her to the throne room. Abram had already been summoned and was on his way.

Sarai's husband entered the great hall of the Egyptian king with his eyes lowered. This was a normal precaution, but in truth he was relieved to be able to avoid meeting Sarai's eyes. Well he might be. Abram bowed his head, and waited for the Pharaoh to speak. Some enraged part of Sarai urgently wanted to see him punished for what he had done. She had to hold herself back from falling at the Pharaoh's feet and begging him to impose the death penalty after all.

She stood frozen beside him, looking at Abram, bent low on the ground.

'What have you done?' Pharaoh boomed dangerously at Abram, who looked up, startled and afraid for his life at the rumbling threat in the voice. 'Why did you tell me she was your sister?' Abram glanced anxiously at Sarai, uncertain as to how much exactly the Pharaoh now knew. She felt disinclined to help. 'Why did you not tell me she was your wife? Do you think I need to steal other men's wives? I have not touched her. Take her, and get out. Go.'

The Pharaoh's men accompanied them back to their camp and waited as they pulled up the stakes and prepared to leave.

'Does he want us to leave the gifts he gave us, do you think?' Abram asked Sarai.

'I don't think he cares very much, but I doubt he will want anything from you. Let us take the wealth he gave us. You risked a great deal for it, my brother.' ─────────

───────── I maintained my silence, not deigning to reveal my part in securing the soundness of the future mother of my nation. Damn fools, both of them, him and her. But he, at least, was wretched with his disobedience. She actually believed that she herself had prevented the Pharaoh from violating her. Abram, in a moment of rebellion, had wanted to subvert my power and take human control of fertility even if it meant another man's seed impregnating Sarai with my promise of posterity. I would not forget his recklessness with my word. But Sarai remained stolid in her disbelief. Abram believed but wished I were not his master; Sarai would not even recognise my hand in the affairs of my creatures. It was galling. Very galling.

I afflicted the Pharaoh with his inability to penetrate the woman. He withered at my command, not her words, nor at his sense of propriety. How easily the human supposes the world to be under their control. What faith their lack of faith gives them. But I was too angry to make a display of my displeasure. I would bide my time with Sarai. Abram I tormented with my angry silence. I was learning the ways of love. I turned my face from him and let him stew in his own shame and guilt at his betrayal of his Lord —————

—————   They left Egypt and returned to the Negev with a burden of wealth that was matched only by the weight of Abram's guilt and Sarai's misery at how it had been obtained. They travelled in stages back the way they had come, setting up and striking camp, heading northward, back, Abram announced, to the high ground between Bethel and Ai, though for all Sarai cared they might have been burrowing deep into the bowels of the earth. She became – how did the others put it to each other? – unwell.

Abram appeared to have returned to something like his old self. Troubled, deeply troubled, but solid and strong, a leader of the group with a direction and a purpose. He was almost the man who had been Sarai's youthful husband when life and love had completed themselves for her in him.

But she did not care what conclusions he had come to in his mind, how the adventure in Egypt had resolved whatever needed resolving in his soul. She did not even care when no tent was raised for her, and she took her place once again beside Abram in his bed. He was gentle, though he did not make love to her; but nor did Sarai did care about that, neither the one nor the other. She had thought herself a stranger in a strange land when she lay, feeling discarded, in the Pharaoh's arms while his satiny fingers played over her breasts. She thought then that she could get no further from her life, but now, as the distance grew between Egypt and herself and she lay once again in the dark strong arms of her Abram, she was more asunder than the stars from the sands of the desert. It seemed as if the sweet Egyptian fingers on her flesh were the last thing that had held her in place in the world, and that now she floated away, ungrounded by any human touch. During the night, as they retreated from Egypt, while her body remained stranded in the desert, she lost her connection to it and drifted upwards, into the icy blackness of the night sky, into the bloody, searing heat of the midday sun.

All through that journey back through the Negev, they fed her, washed her, and carried her away from Egypt. She was an empty shell, a shed skin, that Abram and the others treated as if it were still a person, though no gesture was made by her hands, no expression appeared on her face, no voice issued from the husk of her body. She was aware of the vacated space, but she, like the others, could only observe it from a distance, wide-eyed with terror, reaching out with invisible hands to get a purchase on it so that she

might regain her grounding on earth. Even human unhappiness, even the bitter disappointment of lost love and
betrayal was preferable to the floating terror and helplessness
of disembodiment. She had thought that night in Pharaoh's
palace that she no longer wanted to live; now she would
have embraced either life or death with equal gratitude for
rescuing her from this fearfulness, this inhuman statelessness
that she could never before have imagined. I think, if he
had spoken to her, she would even have heard Abram's
lord.

But he did not speak, and for a long time neither life nor
death released her from her agonised isolation. Everything
passes, they say. This is true of life on earth, so far as I can
tell. Everything passes, but nothing entirely goes away.
Conditions change, states alter, circumstances shift, but they
do not disappear. The form transmutes, but the substance
remains, the elements from which the state was made re-
form but retain their potential to re-create what was there
before. There is only so much stuff on earth from which all
things, all flesh, all mind, are made. The particles reshape,
but always the shadow of what they were and what they
could become again remains. What is known stays known.
What has been can be. What could be might be. Everything
passes but nothing ceases. So gradually Sarai regained her
place within her body and among her people, the horror
passed, but now she knew how tenuous the connection was
between herself and the world, how easily it might be
snapped, so that she remained always in a state of dread and
watchfulness. And she knew that she would rather die than
exist in that lonely space again.

She came to herself, as Abram, Lot, his wife and the girls put it, by the time they reached Bethel. Abram returned to the altar he had built in the place between Bethel and Ai and invoked the name of his lord. Sarai's return to health, along with the Pharaoh's refusal to sleep with her was a double cause for calling out his renewed faith to his god. Though the lord was still maintaining his silence, events on earth had confirmed him to Abram, who now reiterated his faith with the scent of barbecued kid moistened with tears of gratitude and penitence. Sarai's Abram had become a passionate lover again, and he would worship his beloved and wait until it graced him with another precious word. Sarai no longer had the energy to feel jealous. She merely watched and began to learn how love lives apart from its object, attaching itself to whatever it might, and enthralling mere humans in its arbitrary grip ─────

───── She was ripe for the taking. But I decided that I did not want her. She was to be nothing more than a vessel between Abram and me. I could have called her name when she was floating free and vulnerable, and she would have heard me, reached out in gratitude for my voice to steady her chaos. But I am a most particular *I am*. I wanted only the devotion, the trust of Abram, my chosen one. I desired – the first desiring I had known – the dyadic *us* that my inventions had invented. The woman was nothing more than the means of securing Abram's love for myself. I had no wish for her mental comfort. She who refused to recognise my power or even my existence would get no succour from me. I left her to herself to know the paltriness, the mere contingency of life on earth without the gift of my voice and the introduction of my purpose. I rejoiced in her lovelessness.

They settled in the land between Bethel and Ai, among the Canaanite and the Perizite peoples who had long inhabited the area, staking their initial claim in the place that was to become their nation according to Abram's lord. Not that they mentioned this to the Canaanite and the Perizite, to whom they were merely a small band of settlers who could, if they were not warlike or greedy, be accommodated and traded with. They knew nothing of Abram's new-fangled god or his territorial intentions.

Abram was robust with faith. Lot, on the other hand, untroubled by any calling from the lord, was beginning to hanker after a life of his own. All his life he had followed and obeyed. It had taken a long time, but eventually even Lot found his wish to please eroded by a desire to see himself as autonomous. Now he was no longer a boy but a man approaching young middle age, with a wife, several mistresses among the Canaanites and a wish to stand in his own light, away from Abram's shadow. When they left Egypt, Abram had separated the herds of sheep, goats and oxen, giving half to his nephew as his own. Now that their wandering seemed to be over, and they had become a set-tled people, they began to experience the difficulties of a sedentary existence, or rather the difficulties that people have when sharing, rather than merely passing through the land.

After the cosiness of *us*, comes *us and them*. Lot's herdsmen began to antagonise those who cared for Abram's beasts, mocking them with their master's sterility.

'They'll be ours soon enough. Why not give them to us now?' they jeered. 'Hey, give us that new calf. New life is wasted on Abram. When the old man dies, it'll come to us anyway. No matter, come to think of it. You keep it for now. You feed it and fatten it, and we'll inherit it.'

Abram's lads complained of the contempt they had to suffer from Lot's people. Abram tried to soothe them, but loyalties divided them into two camps, dangerously eyeing each other, though in their daily existence Lot displayed an elaborate respect for his uncle. The game became too hazardous for a small alien group trying to live in a new land inhabited by real strangers. And Lot's underlying resentment of Abram was not going to stay underground for ever.

'We must not quarrel amongst ourselves,' Abram said, one evening at dinner.

'But, Uncle, when have I ever quarrelled with you?'

'Perhaps we have too much now to be able to share the same territory. You must go and make a life of your own. Look around, choose what land you want. If you want the east, I'll take the west. If the west suits you better, then I'll be content to live in the east.'

This benevolence on Abram's part did not seem to take into account that none of the land was either his or Lot's to divide between them. But the Lord's promise was enough for Abram to regard the indigenous population of Canaanites and Perizites as mere campers on the land of Abram's nation-to-be. Sarai said nothing, but marvelled at the perfect mixture of wisdom and foolishness that mingled in her former love.

The next morning Lot announced that he would take the richly irrigated plain of the Jordan river to the east as his own, leaving Abram with the mountains and desert land of Canaan. He took his wife, his children, his grandchildren, his mistresses, his herds of sheep, goats and oxen and his followers and made permanent camp on the outskirts of Sodom. The cities of the plain were not for Abram, who hated their noise and distraction. The clamour of cities was too great. He needed the silence of the rural night to listen for the word of the Lord, should it ever come to him again. And Lot, though attracted by their energy and sophistication, chose at this time to live near but not within their boundaries. He was torn with wishes frustrated by hesitancy, his father's son in his desires, but his grandfather's adopted boy in his fearfulness. He had not grown up well, but how could he, that child of shame and exile? Now, for all Abram's apparent graciousness, he was being exiled once again. Lot was a soul condemned to a boundary life and indecision. The apparent freedom of choice bestowed on him by Abram was a fraud. What real option had Lot but to choose the almost easy life and leave the stony ground of virtue to Abram who wanted it so very much? Lot, that baby Sarai had cherished so much when she feared she had caused the death of love, she now saw might never have had a chance to grow straight and strong, and thus able to covertly

manipulate the world as Sarai's oh-so-righteous, and once –
and still, and still? – oh-so-beloved Abram   —————

—————   *Her* love. Her lifelong knowledge of her
beloved. Only now did she begin to see a glimpse of
Abram's deviousness. And she did not know the half of it.
I knew him through and through, and yet, omniscient as I
am, he still surprised me, still, so politely, challenged me.
Challenged *me*. Such is the deluding power of love: knowing everything isn't enough.

It was time to speak again to my chosen one.

'Abram,' I whispered, in his yearning ear. 'Look all around
you, from where you stand on your mountaintop. Look to
the north, to the Negev, to the east and to the sea. All this
land I give to you and to your offspring for all time.'

Of course, it was his already, since Lot had chosen the
plain of Jordan. But I decided to formalise the arrangement
with a retrospective gift, adding, of course, the promise of
future that I knew Abram wanted above all else. He heard
me, but said nothing. Sulking, I swear.

'I will make your seed like the dust of the ground,' I
coaxed. 'Can a man count the particles of dust? Neither will
your offspring be countable.'

A little devious this promise, but I was dealing with a
devious man. Yes, I reiterated his future, but I also, you will
please note, reminded him from what he had come and who
had made him. Just dust.

And still he remained silent. Who did he think he was?

Me? And yet, and yet, there was something in me that responded to his withholding of himself. It was new for me to taste my own silent rebuke. It even amused me that Abram had learned the trick from me. Very adaptable, these humans. My chosen one chose not to speak to me, as if I were the petitioner, and my promises, my gift of nation-hood, were mere trinkets to placate a sullen lover. She believed that Abram's faith was lost and then restored. But it was a good deal more intricate than that. Abram had never lost his faith. He knew who I was from the moment I first spoke to him. He knew my power. But he also had the temerity, the quiet temerity, to know the extent of his own power. Certainly, I could crush him and his to dust, extinguish him from the fact and the memory of the world; but I could not do that without extinguishing too my light in the world, my image of myself, my beloved. He knew the power of having been chosen and played me with it as Adam and Noah had never thought to do. Is this what they mean by evolution? ————

———— Not long after Lot went his way, Abram spent the night communing with the stars. He returned at dawn to his tent, and announced to Sarai that they were moving south once again.

They made a new permanent settlement in Hebron, by the Oaks of Mamre, and there he built an altar to make sac-rifices to his Lord. Abram was now a bit of a lord himself. They were a wealthy tribe, with an increasing retinue of

followers and, of course, the slaves from Egypt. They lived
well, as if they belonged in that land, and indeed as if the
land belonged to them. Sarai returned to her old task of running the household, no longer the same woman she had
been, but relieved that an approximation of normality had
returned to her life. Human laziness accounts for a good deal
of contentment. Abram built up the herds and traded in the
area, for all the world as if he were a prince of the region. He
developed the look of a substantial man, and if during his
encounters with other traders and breeders he told them of
his Lord, well, everyone had their little ways. No one
minded and no one took very much notice, but every now
and again a small band would arrive and join the settlement,
brought by their household head who had given a more
careful ear to Abram's part-time preaching. Whether they
were convinced by his proclamations of the Lord, whose
attributes seemed few and far between – invisible, silent
except to his chosen one, full of promises but short on delivery – I can't say. More than likely it was something about
Abram himself that attracted them. He existed in a micro-
climate of calm air, confident even in the way his feet
touched the ground as he walked. He seemed so solid, so
certain, so quiet. You might think his god not much good
for anything, but Abram you would want to get to know
better. *That* Abram. The one Sarai had loved for so long as
brother and husband.

And now, seeing him the way others did and she used to,
did she love him? She always loved, would always love what
he had been, who he had been for her, but that was an
Abram of her memory, before the madnesses, before Egypt.

And it was a memorised love, not a living current vibrating through the connective tissue that tied together body and soul. She fed on it during her quiet moments, as a starving prisoner might recall the finest meal he had ever had. A middle-aged woman, recollecting young hands on a young body, whispers in the night, looks passing like secret letters between outsiders who, they were sure, knew nothing of the depth of feeling they had for each other. Sarai cherished the physical memories of her young husband, and also the remembered safety of her strong brother, the idol of her childish dreams, the apotheosis of everything a person might become. Yes, yes, all that. But did she love him now? No. Yes. How little wisdom age brings to one's understanding of one's feelings. To her understanding of her feelings. She was numb, and yet it was a numbness that was underlain by something she could not quite retrieve but which had not entirely disappeared. Perhaps there was a residue of love for the love she had had for him. Perhaps she loved him, always had and always would, then passionately, now numbly. I cannot say. She did not feel love, but does that mean she did not love him? Yes. No. No matter, they were married. Completely married. They rubbed along, an old couple, living the life they were supposed to lead, except for the children they did not have, and the grandchildren they would not have.

And it happened that four kings from the land between the two rivers, that Mesopotamia where, long ago, Sarai had begun her life, made an alliance and decided to make war on the rebellious client princes of Sodom and Gomorrah and

the other rulers of the cities of the plain around the Dead
Sea. The rebellion failed and the princes of Sodom and
Gomorrah ended up in bitumen pits, while their conquerors
sacked the cities. On their way home, the triumphant army
passed Lot's encampment, on the outskirts of the city of
Sodom. They stole what they did not destroy and carried
Lot and his family off with them as their prisoners. There
was always trouble around Sodom and Gomorrah, and Lot,
as if it were irresistible, had chosen the cities of the plain to
make a new life of his own.

When people stay still, war begins. They had decided to
stay still, and now the history of the region they inhabited
became their present context. A new fact of life. And once
again Abram showed himself to be remarkably adaptable to
change – so strange, Sarai thought, remembering the troubled boy lodged in her mind. When they had had to become
travellers, he learned trade and animal husbandry. When
they became settlers, he learned war. Her Abram gathered
men around him, armed them and trained them as if he had
been born to military command, turning herdsmen into a
troop of fearsome fighting men that marched north up to the
land of Dan, to rescue the nephew he had so recently sent
away. Apparently, war is not so difficult to learn. Apparently,
necessity can make warriors of us all. And blood, the blood
of Terah that flowed in Lot's veins as well as Abram's, was
worth spilling blood over. Well, what else was there to do?
Lot was family. He and his children were all the family
Abram and Sarai had beyond the unreasonable promise of
Abram's unreasonable lord. What future was there for the
house of Shem if its youngest and only fertile members were

allowed to die? It seemed that Abram did not trust in his god quite enough to leave him to sort the problem out. Abram returned, established by his latest works as a warrior and a prince of the territory, with his family intact. The surrounding leaders recognised him as one of them rather than risk him rising against them, and a treaty was proposed. What more could any man want, especially a man so afraid of doubt as Abram? They received a visit from Melchizedek, High Priest and King of Jerusalem who blessed Abram to El Elyon, the local Lord High God of the gods. Sarai's Abram, now all politics and cunning, abjured the spoils of war in the name of the Lord, the Most High God, which sounded to her ears like a canny compromise of deities, from this man who had once known only the simplicities of carving and emotional distress. She looked in wonder at her long-loved husband, now a man of the world, a worldly man, and she supposed that he had found a way at last to do without the lord of vague promises who for so many years had ridden on his back ————————

———————— After the war, lagging behind as ever, I appeared to my chosen one in a night vision.

'Fear not, Abram,' I whispered my word in his ear like a freshening wind, 'I am your shield. Your reward shall be very great.'

A little late, I grant, a touch *post facto*.

'O my Master, Lord,' he said, barely looking about him, and in a tone of voice that seemed to me somewhat to undercut the reverential terms he used to address me. My first taste, I believe, of sarcasm. 'What can you possibly give me when for all your promises, and my worldly success I will die childless?'

His worldly success? Did he think he had become a warrior all on his own? Did he think he could be anything or anyone in the world without my assistance? Yes, he did. Why, I saw him smile to himself when I first spoke, as if he thought (and wouldn't I know what he thought?) he alone had triumphed against the foreign kings. As if I, the Lord, I am that I am, needed him. Ha! Ha, I say.

'You will have a son that issues from your loins,' I whispered in his ear. 'Look up, Abram. Look into the sky and count the stars. Can you number them? That is how numerous your heirs shall be.'

It was a fine cloudless sky that night. Abram looked and dreamed of a posterity that might memorialise his worldly success. I pressed my claim. 'I am the Lord who brought you out of Ur to come to this land your offspring will inherit.'

'My Lord, how shall I know that this will be my land?'

Always just a little sceptical. Always needing a deal. He was almost mine again, but these humans need ritual, treaties and such, to feel secure. A gentlemen's agreement just won't work with them. A formal covenant was required.

'Bring me a three-year-old heifer, a three-year-old she goat and a three-year-old ram.' The old three times three trick. I don't know what it is about the number three but it always works a treat. 'Oh, and get a turtledove and a young pigeon,' I added, just for complexity's sake. I hurriedly invented a rite. Cleave them, pass between the parts, that sort

of thing. Divisions into two is another good way of getting
the attention of my creatures. A pantomime ensued, and
before Abram could decide that the whole thing was stuff
and nonsense, I sent him into a deep, receptive trance and
intoned both the good news and the bad.

'Your offspring, as numerous as the stars, will become
strangers in a strange land, enslaved and afflicted for four
hundred years. But I will punish the nation that does this to
them, and they will emerge a rich people. And you, Abram,
father of the nation, you will grow to a great old age and live
in contentment.' At which I performed some hocus-pocus
with a flaming torch and a smoking brazier and made the
covenant that would make Abram finally my own.

'To your seed I have given this land from the river of
Egypt to the great river Euphrates,' I boomed. That, I
thought, should do it.

What more reassurance could the man want, apart from
the actual achievement of my promise in the form of a flesh-
and-blood son? But I had to keep something in reserve. I
had to have something ————

———— Another vision. By the standards of Abram's
god they were coming thick and fast now. Four times this
lord had visited, four times he had promised, over the passing years. And how the years had passed. Decades. So many
promises, and still no child. Of course, when Sarai was newly
beloved by Abram, she, too, had been full of promise, and
what had emerged from that? Whether Abram was so weak,

so hungry for future, that he had to invent the supernatural
to fulfil his empty longings, or whether this lord of his actually existed, he was still Sarai's greatest rival. Either Abram
and the house of Shem were all she had, or the terrible
coldness, the vast emptiness would descend, and she did not
believe she could live any longer in so vacant a world. It had
become a matter of life and death for Sarai. She saw that desolation stalked her, as it had stalked Haran, and perhaps,
after all, it was she who had taken over his despair and would
come to his conclusion. She had such thoughts. If all the
good in her life was over, the love, the belonging finally
seen to be irrevocable, what was there to continue for?
Where was the point? If Haran could end the intolerable, so
could she. It began to seem a courageous, incisive act. Or at
least an act that she could perform. Abram had his belief;
Sarai had the possibility of ending her life.

Histrionic, you might say. What gave her the impression
that her life had to be so different from that of the rest of the
world? Love, I think. The wall of love that had surrounded
her, imprisoned her even, the adored brother whose eyes
were opened and became the adoring husband. Should she
complain about such early fortune in a world where very
few feel so cherished for so much of their lives? She had had
love and had it doubled for so long. Is lack of love or loss of
love the worse condition? No, love, love itself is to blame.
Love, the idea, the existence of the idea, makes us histrionic
whether we possess it and lose it, or never have it at all.

Full with years though Sarai was, a child well loved, a
woman for so long well loved, she was now quietly suicidal
in her loveless desert, and bitter with jealousy at this lord,

her ghostly adversary who offered Abram the only thing in all the world that could transcend the craving for love – a presence in the future to refute the blankness of individual death —————

————— In the beginning was the Word and the Word was . . . what was the word? It was, it must have been *I am*, and yet the power of that word weakened, I felt the *I am* reduce as my experience of humanity increased. It began to ring hollow, no more than a name among names, and a forgotten name at that. They certainly forgot it, and even I had to dig deep into my recollection of the moment of separation from eternity to regain a sense of the enormity of my Word. Even then, it was only a recollection, not the vivid thrill of knowing myself as being, having been, always to be, within the everlasting present of eternity.

A new word took root, not *the* word, not the word in the beginning, but a word embedded in humanity, an inadvertent, but of course in retrospect inevitable consequence of the gift of *I am*, freely given to them. And, from the seed I had planted on the earth that I had created, it grew towards me, its tendrils quivering to grasp and twist itself around whatever it may find, and finding me, it wound itself around my immaterial being until I too was held fast by the word that was none of my making. Love, love, love, love. Not my word. Not of me, of *I am* wrenched from eternity, complete, undivided, whole, without need, without desire, without longing. It wormed its way into my perfection, this word of humanity, and left a cavity in the flawless *I am* that ached to be filled. I had learned so much from my creatures, and now I learned the anguish of desire. I learned love.

And I hated what I had made.

And I . . . I . . . I . . . the Lord, the Creator, the Eternal, the Singularity, the Complete, the *I am* – I craved the love of Abram ————

———— Abram was all patience, waiting at Mamre for his lord's promise to come true. To all the world he looked as though he led the life of a rich respected leader of his clan, a warrior, a trader. It was a life well lived. But Sarai knew that he was only waiting for his lord to speak again, for the promise of offspring to be fulfilled. The present was mere breathing, keeping on in anticipation of the future.

For Sarai there was only patience, too. There was no future, only a present that stretched beyond the bounds of endurance, to be broken only by the whim of her husband's phantom. Over time her patience became as pitiless as the desert itself. One night, after more than a decade of waiting since the last promise of posterity to her husband, she sought him out in the grove where he had built his altar to his lord, and where he walked and listened for him in the cool of the evening.

'Abram, my husband, have you noticed how the years have passed? Do you hear the sound of the multitude of your descendants intoning your name? Do you hear the sound of even one small offspring calling you Papa?'

Abram's face darkened, but he continued to walk, speaking quietly and swiftly to her with his head down, as if he might detest the sight of her.

'I trust in the Lord,' he said. 'The Lord's time is not our time. You can't understand. Please leave me.'

Sarai kept pace with her husband.

'But our time is our time, and it is all we have. Has it crossed your mind that far from giving you what he promised, your lord has withheld it? What *I* know about your lord is that he has prevented me from bearing children – that is, if he has any power at all. And yes, I certainly believe this god of yours has power, not just because of the empty ache of my arms which have never held my child, but because I know about him.'

'Foolishness, you talk nonsense, woman.'

'No, my dear, let me tell you about this lord of yours.'

'What can you know?'

'Stories, my love, I know stories. I know stories that women know, that women tell each other in the seclusion of their time of uncleanliness, when the blood flows and the men keep away. Your lord is an old story. You are not the first to be chosen, did he tell you that? Your lord is capricious, dealing life and death, bestowing misery and hope, enticing and withdrawing like any flirtatious girl who would have her way with the world.'

'Do you think I would listen to women's stories?'

'Yes, you will listen. I will tell and you will listen, because if your lord does not prevent me from speaking, there is nothing for you to do but hear me, and if he does stop my words you will know I tried to speak the truth.'

For a moment they waited in the singing silence of the grove.

'So,' Sarai said softly. 'I will speak.'

Abram quickened his pace and walked ahead of her, but she knew that he was listening.

She told him about the creator god who had made a world that was a desert surrounding a garden where he planted the first man and woman to whom he gave, with hardly a thought, consciousness, companionship, dominion, but from whom he withheld the source of power – the knowledge of good and evil, or so he called it. And when these two began to live fully, to experience themselves fully, to learn about the world, good and evil, autonomy, the nature of reproduction, the nature of companionship, their nature, not his, he punished them. He sent them out of the garden of peace and quiet and easeful tedium to the surrounding desert, which was also of his making. He created difficulty, hardship, pain, this god, this vengeful, secretive god with an agenda of his own. But the man and woman survived, chose to survive. Thrived, even, in the difficult desert. They took what they had been given and made a life for themselves. So the world went its own way, the way of good and evil, the way of everything that is and can be, and the god continued to punish and outlaw, as each of his attributes was taken from him by the resourcefulness of the creature he created. Humanity went about its own business, taking what it had been given – self-consciousness and fertility – and doing the best and worst with them.

She told him how finally, in an act of petulance, this unbodied god had destroyed everything he had made, disgusted with the flesh that humanity had learned to live with for better or worse. How he had wiped out everything and everyone, but saved a single man and his family, a docile man who had obeyed the voice, who was no more than good enough in his generation, and who never once questioned the destruction of his fellow beings, of all the life that had learned to thrive on the earth, who saved himself, but who, eventually perhaps haunted by conscience, by human conscience, had eaten of another tree of good and evil and lived the life he had been saved for in a mist of alcoholic forgetfulness.

She told him how this testy god had turned his back on humanity, and how humanity managed well enough without him. How they learned to reclaim the desert, to water it into a garden of their own devising, to live in groups as best they could, and to improve their conditions by their own innovation. How they began to build shelters and community against the vagaries of the earth and then to make monuments to their own survival. How out of nothing they began to imagine a future they could not be in, but to which they could leave a legacy to let each generation know that human hands had made their life possible. And the god, fearing for the loss of power over what most terrified and cowed humanity, had confused and scattered them. Separated them, isolated them. Set group against group by estranging them from one another. Instilled dissent and incomprehension. This jealous, vicious god punished and divided and diminished what he had made, for making a life of their own, for managing well enough without him. That was Abram's lord, who wished above all to control his creatures, who ordered them to multiply but discovered too late that life had a life of its own, and who in his omnipotence could do nothing with it but destroy it.

And now, rather than admit the defeat of wiping out the world that was supposed to mirror him and didn't, this god looked for another docile man, a man in shock at the turmoil of his life, a man who craved certainty, who quailed at extinction, but who could imagine the repetition of his name by future generations and found compensation only in that thought. This time, the god narrowed his focus to that man alone, easier to master, let the world go its way, he decided, develop a single people from a single person, separate them from the rest of humanity, make the dutiful man promises, bait him with the honour of having been chosen, entice him with posterity, as if posterity were not already his entitlement, and then prevent him from having a child. Keep this hungry man to himself by keeping him hungry. Promise and withhold. It was a small project for the creator of an entire world, but who can say whether that world was not just a small project itself? If this was the wisest god, the world had best go on its way alone, except for those who found such autonomy intolerable, for those who craved certainty and could never find it in fallible humanity. They made the world a great thing, and a single creator their all and everything, so that when they heard his voice, and of course they *would* hear his voice, they knew they were chosen, were in the presence of certainty and were safe.

'Your lord, Abram,' Sarai finished, 'promises you a destiny, and stops up my womb. He demands your love and leaves me bereft of it. He tells you he loves you and transforms your human life, your only life, into arid waiting. This lord fears humanity, fears its capacity to make connection. He is a separator, a baffled, angry solitary who cannot bear the results of his thoughtless creating. He is an infant who gave birth to parents whose interest in each other he cannot tolerate. He loves you and I love you, yet neither of us has given you hope beyond the grave. He fears that giving you a child will weaken his hold on you. I don't. I am stronger than him, Abram. I am life. I am of the world. He is not. I will give you a child, whatever the consequences, because I love you and I have my own need, and my love and my need are greater than his. We do not need your god, we need a child-bearing woman, Abram. Take my slave, Hagar, the child of the slave the Pharaoh gave to me. You remember the Pharaoh, your last half-defiant bid for independence both from your lord and from me? Take Hagar as your concubine, make a child with her who will be my child too, because I will it. Let us laugh in the face of this god. You do not need your lord, you need a young woman with a ripe womb. The child will be ours, Abram, because we choose it to be so, just as I was the chosen daughter of Emtelai. We will make our own future.'

And Abram said not a word. He did not try to silence Sarai as she told the women's story of the creator god, nor did he look at her until she had finished and silence returned to the grove where he had built an altar to his Lord. Sarai waited in the silence, having won or lost her old and only love, having won or lost her bid for life.

Finally, he turned.

'Can we?' he asked, piercing her with a bright, black stare.

'It is the way of the world,' she said.

Sarai lay alone in the bed she and Abram shared, savouring her triumph. He had chosen her over his lord, and joined her in a rebellion against impotence and destiny. Which meant that for the first time since she was thirteen years old, Abram was in the arms of another woman. A lush, exotic woman, just far enough from girlhood to ensure a ready womb for Abram's seed, for him to make his own earthly destiny. Hagar had been a gift of the Pharaoh to Sarai; now she was a gift from Sarai to her husband. A weapon in the battle for his love, a vessel that would carry the deepest desires of both into the world of flesh and bone.

Sarai shadowed the love-making of her husband and the girl with her own body, with the memory of his youthful love for her as her guide. She felt Abram's imagined hand on Hagar's breast caressing her own, his lips gentle on Hagar's mouth pressed on hers, his fingers separating the moist lips between Hagar's legs testing her own readiness to receive him, his seed pumping into Hagar's depths finding a long-lost, long-bereft egg of her own to fertilise. In this way, the love and the child would be hers, although the body was not. Hagar was the ghost of the girl that Sarai had been, vanishing the decades, rectifying the slippage of love, and the absence of life that she had suffered. In Hagar, Sarai renewed herself.

When he had finished, Abram left Hagar and returned immediately to Sarai waiting in their bed, to spend the remainder of the night with her. Abram took his wife in his arms and held her against his beating heart, as if his passion had been spent on her. He kissed her slowly, his head buried in her neck, and murmured sleepy gratitude, as if it was with her that he had cried out and into her that he had shuddered life. They slept close and collusive, while in another room in the servants' quarters Hagar lay unaccompanied and impregnated ————

———— And now, having taught me love, my fine creation offered me yet a new experience, and pity was added to my repertoire of feeling. She did not weep or complain, this young creature wrenched from her world and now used to salve the pain of the woman and the longing of the man, and to wrest from me what was mine to give or take. I had not noticed human anguish before: I, being of eternity, had had no capacity to feel the suffering of the creatures I had made. I dealt in punishment, retribution, in correcting the faults I perceived in a perverse humanity that found ever more devious ways to escape and evade my authority. What other means had I but suffering to promote my ascendancy? I did not feel what they felt, only saw what they did. It took this single girl, and my own newly developed discomfort in love, to perceive at last what suffering felt like. Though she did not weep, I found a place inside her as vast and empty and cold as my own eternity. A place too terrible to be the internal landscape of such a small and vulnerable creature, where loneliness howled like an arctic wind eroding her young heart. She was too frail, too human to share my icy eternity, and yet I saw in her unhappiness my own terrible existence, and I discovered pity.

And I discovered something more terrible still. Wrested into pity, perceiving at last suffering through this singular girl, did not alter or diminish in any way my love for Abram. Pity for Hagar did not convert into love for her. I loved Abram still. It was him I longed for, though I knew that Hagar needed and deserved my love so much more. Having chosen, I found myself unable to unchoose, omnipotent Lord though I might be. I was as helpless in the face of what humanity had infected me with as they. A prey to feeling that refused to adjust itself to rational thought, to reason and convenience. I would have loved Hagar, but I could not. I had only pity for her. Love was locked on the source of her pain. What had Abram done to deserve my love? Nothing. What were his special qualities? None. Except that he had longed for me before he knew of my existence, had called me to him with his need for certainty. Here, at last, was my mirror, a surface so polished by insecurity and longing that it created something to reflect out of its craving to fill its blank surface. Abram caught me by seeing me. He was my chosen one because he had chosen me. I wanted to be implicated in his life and the life of his seed that was mine to give or withhold. I wanted, at last, a tribe of my own, which saw me vividly in its past, present and future. I wanted a past, present and future. Eternity, it turned out, was not enough. I wanted to be loved in time.

And had I learned also to hate? I knew that Sarai was my only rival, that her capacity to fulfil Abram's desires was the only danger. She might have satisfied him with fleshly love, companionship and the child that would have made me unnecessary. The world would have been enough for Abram whose wish for mystery and meaning would have been assuaged by the proliferation of his generations through time, the progeny of his progeny, the continuation of the begettings, that world without end. What else could I do, I who had never before been chosen by my creatures, but block his route to contentment? Yes, I hated Sarai. She chose the world, when, like Abram, she might have chosen me out of her need. Yet something stopped her, something remained firmly of the world. For her the world was flesh and blood, flesh from blood. She chose the world as meaning. She opposed me with the very means of reproduction that I had burdened her kind with. She was the only thing that stood in the way of my complete possession of my beloved Abram. She was the way of the world ————————

———————— Sarai suffered her victory as victors must. Hagar, with a child growing in her womb, discovered her own power. She may have been gifted by the Pharaoh to this wandering tribe, and may have been gifted by her mistress to the bed of Abram, but she had roused the desire of the husband of her mistress and made his child, had created and was nurturing its life, as her elderly, barren mistress had never been able to do. She lived now, with servants taking every care of her, in the main part of the house, a temporary treasure, a carrier of the fortune of the house of Shem. She was young, she was good-looking, she was fertile. She no longer rose from her couch when Sarai came to see how she was.

She lolled, sleepy-eyed, savouring her triumph over her mistress, shrugging at her questions – Had she eaten properly? Was she feeling all right? Could she feel the baby kicking yet? – as if to say, what business is it of yours? Sarai tasted Hagar's contempt and saw her belly swell. The old can comfort themselves that it is blind foolishness for the young to flaunt their youth, their beauty, their fertility in the face of age and incapacity. The old know what is to come for the young who taunt them, how accidental and momentary their triumph is, that time, and not much of it, will take care of the insult. But it is a cold comfort. And Sarai discovered that playing God at his own game gave her all God's disadvantages. She could manipulate the world, but she could not participate in it. The world swelled with the life that she had willed into being, and mocked her for being unable to indulge in her achievement with any of her senses but that of sight. She could only look. Wanting a child for Abram, for herself, she had not taken into consideration the pain of having to observe someone else actually living the experience. Watching someone else bear her child was, after all, more than she could bear. Hagar's insolent eyes told her more about herself than she wanted to know. And, like God, Sarai discovered a desire to destroy what she had caused to be made.

'I want her out of the house. I want her out of our territory,' she screamed at Abram.

'But she's practically a child. And she's pregnant.' Sarai heard what he did not say: pregnant with my child.

'Have you no pity?' he begged.

Sarai was pitiless.

'This is your fault. You and your lord can pity her. For me she has nothing but contempt and knowing eyes.'

'But you –'

'It is your fault. Your fault,' she shouted, drowning out his unreasonable and irrelevant rationality.

Abram, perhaps the first among men to wish for a quiet life in the midst of the earthy and conflicting demands of his women, withdrew from the debate. He shook his head and raised his hands in a gesture of submission. 'She is your slave-girl,' he murmured. 'You must do whatever you think is right.'

And, thus absolved, he left the young woman who carried his only child to his fuming, guilt-enraged wife.

Sarai could do no more about her behaviour to Hagar than Hagar could do about her innately youthful triumph over her mistress. They were both prisoners of human conflict, of wishes perversely come true, of the accomplishment of desire at the cost of peace of mind. They might have seen each other as their own selves shifted in time, as connected by suffering whose difference was no more than random, as puppets choreographed by mere circumstance. But their emotions colluded with the way of the world to keep them apart, to make each feel the other to be inimical to their own gratification. For all her belief in her capacity to will a child of Abram's into being from whatever source and make it their own, Sarai now saw Hagar as a weapon in the armoury of Abram's lord, a turncoat in the battle between herself and him. Perhaps she had even acted against her own interests, unknowingly in the interest of the lord, should he exist, in gifting Hagar's fertility to her husband. Winning the battle, she had perhaps lost it irretrievably. Now Abram would have a child and a woman, and the child was not Sarai's and the woman was not her.

The pampering stopped, and Hagar was isolated from both her former life and her new one. She lived in her room, unvisited, belonging to and the concern of no one. As her loneliness grew, she began to understand what was happening to her, and Sarai came to fix that understanding in her mind.

'We have found a wet-nurse. When the child is born it will be taken from you immediately. You will return to your duties. You will not speak to the child. You will have nothing to do with it. As a matter of fact, it may be better if we sold you out of the household. We will see.'

It was not that Sarai had forgotten about her own birth mother whose name she never knew. On the contrary, the thought rose incessantly to her waking and sleeping mind. A faceless concubine had carried her and then conveniently died, causing no embarrassment to the family that took the unformed infant and made her theirs, almost theirs. Sarai felt no sympathy for this echo of her own beginnings. Instead a knot of cruelty formed inside her at the memory of it, and swelled until Sarai could contain it no more. She rejoiced in the desolation of the girl, in her forthcoming anguish as the child she carried was snatched from her and she was sent away from it for ever. Or perhaps, Sarai wondered, she might allow her to remain, obliged to watch the child grow, never knowing what Sarai herself had always known, that it was not entirely a part of the family that surrounded it with their wall of love. These thoughts were not willed, they were not even quite consciously registered, but they were indulged in like half-understood dreams and unreasonable fantasies, floating about in her mind bathed in the nurturing amniotic fluid of a cruelty that had lain dormant since early childhood in the minute cracks between her love for the family of Shem and her fear that she did not really belong to them. She had no power then to punish them for not being hers, or, more obscurely, for making her theirs and withdrawing her from where she truly belonged, but now, all these years on, providing she did not examine herself, she could exact retribution from Hagar. Perhaps that was what she had wanted all along: to punish. To punish the lost and the dead, to punish Abram, and to punish his lord. Her childlessness had provided the opportunity: it was what had made her all these years and at last, potent as a god. Well, she was only human.

So far from the beginning, so far from the garden of the eternal present. From the knowing nothing, feeling only the breath of the passing wind on the external boundaries of one's being. Loss. From that moment on, loss. You would think we might adjust to it, so soon is it part of our existence, so much is it the essence of our existence. And yet for some it seems that loss sensitises them to itself, so that they quail at the slightest encounter with it, at the merest indication of its possibility, until, finally, every good threatens them with its potential loss, and all they can experience is fear. Until, indeed, all experience is fear of loss ————

———— How difficult these humans make life for themselves. How they scrape and dig away at themselves until they find the intolerable murk they might have left well alone. Always in search of self-disgust and always finding it as they scratch away the layers which are all that protect them from their reality. What do they expect to find in all that blood and ordure? They look for gold and find shit. What else? They are matter. That is the truth, their crushing truth. The more they look, the more they find matter, deeper and deeper, and the mess that matter is, and their minds revolt at the truth of themselves. Poor minds, unfit for the reality they are made of.

My fault, I suppose, but I did not know that mind and reality were so inimical. Mind was all the reality I knew. And why should I feel pity for them? Their minds were supposed to reflect mine, to turn away from the accident of their embodiment, the clumsy necessity of creation, to turn a blind eye to the matter of their existence and to dwell on me, on the glory of my immaterial perfection. But flesh and blood were too strong for them, and their minds, perverse human minds, turned on themselves and tried to shine a light on their condition. I gave them too much and not enough. And their reality, which was not mine, turned against me, gave them a place of their own to stand. Neck deep in shitty matter, to be sure, but a place none the less. These sorry sacks of blood and pus called the world theirs, called their realm of predestined decay beautiful, interpreted their own insignificant doom as tragic, and reworked the necessary drudgery of feeding, defecating and reproducing into a high old destiny.

And I longed for them. I had eternity. I had a perfect solitude. I was not sullied by material being. I had no need to strive for anything. I lacked nothing. And yet I watched them struggle against necessity, against the blackness that would consume each and every one of them, rendering all their thoughts, dreams and imaginings to blank nothing, and I was moved. These little lives, snuffed out in less than a breath of my eternity, were so engaged, so busy with their fleeting, hopeless existence.

And out of the brief and pointless span of their lives, they had invented meaning. There is no meaning in eternity, in constancy, in perfect singularity. Meaning was a wonder they had created for themselves, out of desperation, to conceal the blankness, the void over which they walked with every step of their lives. I had no need of meaning, and yet this redundant fantasy that my poor creation created, disturbed and threatened me, and I realised that if I were to be anything at all to these humans, I had to become their meaning. But more than that, I discovered that if I were to be anything to myself, beyond blank perfection, I needed them to become my meaning.

It was Sarai I had to overcome, and she had given me the means to do it in the child growing in Hagar's belly. So when Hagar tried to run away, to return to her own people, I stopped her with promises of future. Her son would never be the son of Sarai. Hagar had to remain in Sarai's presence and the son grow before her eyes so that she and Abram would know they had failed in their bid to take the world from me. Ishmael would be *other* in their camp, a wild child, raging at his condition of unbelonging, a constant reminder of the mess humans made when they tried to have the world their own way. Ishmael would be Sarai's pain, the alternative that was no alternative. And Abram would look on the boy and wonder about the son I had promised him. He would have the son of his flesh, but not the child of my promise. Love and longing outweighing pity, as it does for humans, I sent Hagar back to suffer Sarai's abuse and Abram's neglect and create the conditions for her bellicose son to punish Abram and Sarai with the consequences of rebellion. Had I, by now, learned the full complement of human characteristics: love, longing, pity, hate and now cruelty? How would I know?

Still, there was something left of *I am*: and I let time, of which I had so very much, of which they had so little, pass.

LAUGHTER

Then Abraham fell upon his face, and laughed, and said in his heart, Shall a child be born unto him that is an hundred years old? And shall Sarah, that is ninety years old, bear? And Abraham said unto God, O that Ishmael might live before thee! And God said, Sarah thy wife shall bear thee a son indeed; and thou shalt call his name Isaac: and I will establish my covenant with him for an everlasting covenant, and with his seed after him.
GENESIS 17:17

Therefore Sarah laughed within herself, saying, After I am waxed old shall I have pleasure, my lord being old also?
GENESIS 18:12

The world had another trick up its sleeve to show Sarai. If you do not succumb to despair, you succumb to life. It is the worst of all the losses. The anguish is weathered by time, the intolerable becomes bearable, the pain mutates into a mere background ache. It is the moment when life goes on, when you know the truth, the outcome, the fact, and yet the breath continues, sleep overcomes you at night, your eyes open in the morning and you rise with the day, you eat from hunger, you drink from thirst and find there is relief and even transient pleasure in both. You have not died from despair, and therefore you will live. After a while, you do not even notice how terrible such a loss of loss is.

Abram and Sarai lived a kind of peace, a sort of short-term eternity. They had challenged the Lord and in some way had won. Silence had fallen on Abram's inner ear. There were no more promises, no more enticements for him to look beyond the world around him for meaning in his life. A son had been born, a life had been made, a new generation could be imagined in the future of which he could not be a part. No more could be asked of a life. Sarai had given him all that a man could hope for. She had given him back his world, the only one he could be sure of. And if the child were not Sarai's own, he was still of the house of Shem, fathered by a man of the house of Shem, as she was. There was enough of both of them in the boy. They had done what they could do and made a future without assistance from the lord of so many unkept promises. Sarai had brought Abram back to reality, and now they both lived in it, together, life going on, for better or worse.

Reason prevailed, and the child was not taken from his mother. Hagar and Ishmael lived in their own rooms of the house, and the boy was brought daily to spend time with his father. Sarai kept a distance, and no longer tormented the young woman who had assuaged Abram's dynastic terrors. But, from her distance, she watched with wonder as Ishmael grew to boyhood. It was as if the boy had caught the awkward, troubled young man she remembered Abram once to have been. Dark-browed and uneasy in his own skin. But for Ishmael this was not a phase he passed through, it was the essence of himself. Even as a toddler, the world and he collided, as if they were inimical. He crashed and stamped around, elbowing obstacles out of his way that did not seem to be in the way of others. Unable to rest, it seemed, he was never still, always in search of the new, never content with the present. He fought against sleep, refusing to allow himself to relax however tired he became, stopping only when he dropped from exhaustion. He was not a lovable child, and Sarai was not unhappy to see it was so. He resisted the invitation of adult arms, even those of his mother, as if some danger lurked in embrace. He was, however, more alive than any child Sarai had ever seen. Fidgety with life, forever displacing himself in the world with dark, disordered energy.

What could be done had been done. Abram and Sarai were full with years, life was no more for the making, it had been made. It was there, spread out in memory, so they could see what had become of them. They had known love and loss, security and despair, and discovered that all those things were survivable; the best and the worst. Now they lived with each other, the keeper of each other's story, only their own version of the other, it was true, but the sole witnesses of each other's life. Their existence became regular and even gentle, neither disturbing the other with dissatisfaction. If they thought their own thoughts, they did not trouble each other with them, and the thoughts no longer demanded action in the world.

The year Ishmael was born, Abram planted an orchard of pomegranate trees in the glade at Mamre, and when they had grown he set a tent in their shade where he could spend his days watching the world go by and offer it refreshment on its journey. Now they would stop still, pleased to do so, and allow life to pass, pausing on its way to tell a tale or two in return for hospitality. Very likely, the

Orchard Hotel was the first purpose-built traveller's inn, and much appreciated it was, not just by wayfarers who rested, ate and drank with the elderly couple but by the elderly couple too, who had, it seemed, at last devised still-ness for themselves. A way of being old and waiting for their lives to come to a conclusion ⸻

⸻   As if I would have no say in it. As if mere decision was all there was to be done. And as if, in this telling of a story – both tellings – I were not having my say. As if my say, indeed, were not the story itself. The story's mine, not hers, never was. The interruption is the narrative, the inter-rupter is the narrator. As if her story could be the story. I am the interruption and the narrative. I am the Word and the maker of time. I am the commencement and the conclusion.

And yet, and yet, beside all that, despite the power of the beginning and the end, I had discovered from these humans the inconclusive middle: the wish, the desire, the longing that muddles the clean divisions of my creation. I found myself wanting. And I discovered that the power of wanting can inter-rupt the simplicity of eternity. I had made, in all innocence, in the only innocence that had ever existed in the universe, crea-tures who disrupted the very story of the world with the desire that I had not dreamed of, and had had no desire to know. And as a result, I could not leave that speck of humanity alone. I called it love, after their naming. I called Abram my chosen one, my beloved. Yet what it was I loved in him, I couldn't say. Myself, I suppose, the reflection of myself in his blank compliance. His wilfulness, or rather hers imposed on him, had darkened my reflection. I wanted it back. I wanted my place in the world. From love, from aggravation, from the need to retrieve the woman's subversive narrative, to come to my own conclusion, I could not let Sarai and the world have their way.

This time I made an appearance. I thought something a little extra was needed, and I hadn't felt the earth under my feet – nor my feet – since I wandered in the garden with the first of them. I chose an impressive, light-filled monumental mode for my materialisation.

'I am El Shaddai,' I shimmered at him, catching him unawares, and offering him a name so mysterious that even I didn't know what it meant. Very gratifyingly, he fell flat on his face at my pronouncement. I took it to be fear and trembling in the face of the creator, but I had cause to wonder not much later.

'Walk with me,' I said. 'Be blameless.'

Thus, obliquely, I proposed to overlook his rebellion, his outrageous siding with Sarai against me. A clean slate was what I was offering.

'Be blameless and I will grant my covenant between me and you, and I will multiply you very greatly.'

He was silent. Yes, I know I had granted my covenant before and that he had already multiplied himself, but he needed reminding what was what and who was who. Ishmael was not promising material for a multitude of nations, that much was clear, now the lad was thirteen and not at all improved in character. Abram still needed me, though he stubbornly refused to acknowledge it. I raised the covenantal stakes a notch or two in the face of his continued silence.

'You shall no longer be called Abram, but your name shall be Abraham. I will make you the father of nations, and kings shall come forth from your seed.'

Silence, still silence.

'And I will give you and your seed this land, the whole land of Canaan, as an everlasting holding, and I will be their God.'

Not a word.

'You shall keep my commandments. This is my covenant which you shall keep: every male among you must be circumcised. You will circumcise the flesh of your foreskin as a sign of our covenant, and every male child through the generations shall be circumcised at eight days old.'

When would this man speak? Not even refusal. Nothing, still that sullen silence, even after I demanded that my power be inscribed on his penis, that he prove, after his lapse, that his fertility was mine, his future was mine.

I wanted the sign of my control over one other thing.

'Your wife shall no longer be called Sarai. Sarah is now her name. And I will bless her with your son, and from her will issue nations and kings.'

And finally I got a response. He threw himself on the ground, once again, and lay face down shaking all over his body. At last, I thought, I've got him, he's mine. But then I identified the sound he was making. It took a moment before I recognised it for what it was. There is no laughter in eternity. There are no tears in my realm either, but those tears I had encountered before in my curious creatures, indeed, I learned that tears brought them closer to obedience to me. But though the sound Abraham made was close to weeping, it was quite different, and his sobs were tearless howls of mirth. Not a pretty sound. And whereas tears drew them closer to me, this laughter kept me at a distance, drew a circle about my Abraham as he squirmed on the ground and left me outside, unable to break through the wall of laughter. There were words among his convulsions.

'At my age, I will engender a child and at Sarah's age she will give birth!'

And his grim hee-hawing redoubled. He was not speaking to me, but to some invisible witness who previously had not existed in the world. The god of amusement, the lord of irony. Humankind creates gods for itself at the drop of a hat. And yet, he was not entirely lost to me – I noticed that he spoke of her with the name I had given her. He was bitter, but he was still mine. He kept silence, he laughed, but he did not refuse anything.

Finally, the laughter subsided and he looked up, his eyes damp with mockery.

'I'll settle for what I've got. Let Ishmael thrive.'

Such a divided man, this man who of all humanity I wanted, so weak. Even in his rage at me, throwing his worldly son in my face, he asked for my blessing. He could not commit himself entirely to the world. I could not play the human game of humour, and took his words at face value, as indeed, in part, they were spoken. I would have him trembling again in his uncertain world.

'Sarah will bear you a son. And in memory of your laughter, his name shall be Isaac. My covenant will be with him. As for Ishmael, I will bless him, he will thrive. I will make him a great nation, but not your nation. Your nation, and my people, will come from Isaac, to whom Sarah will have given birth by this time next year.'

With that, and with all the humourless dignity I could muster, I turned off my light in the world and disappeared from the face of the earth.

And why I troubled myself with all this, I don't know. I was the creator. They were mine, of me, in my own image. How could they not love me? How could they resist me? How could such a thing be possible? ————

———— When the madness came again, Sarai realised she had known all along that it would. She woke one morning to a great groaning that seemed to come from all sides of their compound. Abram had been absent most of the previous day and the whole night. When she went outside, she found women ministering to all the men, servants, herdsmen, even the smallest baby boys, every one howling or moaning in pain, while the women held their hands to their faces in shock at what they saw. Abram's personal assistant was sitting in his room crying, while his wife screamed and gesticulated beside him on the bed dipping and squeezing a bloody cloth into a bowl of water.

'What's happened?' Sarai asked the servant. 'Have we been raided in the night?'

He shook his head, only able to stammer out a word or two.

'Abraham . . . this morning . . . ordered . . . all of us . . .'

'Abraham?'

She found Abram, sitting in the opening of his tent in the glade, naked apart from a bloodstained rag across his lap, and rocking back and forth in pain.

'What have you done?'

'The Lord's work,' he answered, looking up at Sarai with a small, sad smile on his face and, wincing, lifted the rag from his lap.

She stared at his mutilation.

'He appeared to me. I saw his light. He promised . . .'

Again he smiled.

'. . . he commanded . . . I and all the men, all the male children must be circumcised. It is to be a sign of our nation. I am renamed Abraham. You are renamed Sarah. Our son, the son we will have this time next year, is to be called Isaac, after my laughter.' He continued to smile, awaiting Sarai's response.

She looked down at the mess between her old husband's legs and nodded. 'At last your lord and I agree about something. If I have a son, I will certainly call him Isaac. What else is there to do but laugh in the face of such craziness?'

She would no longer try to fight against it: the madness was the way of the world too, as much a part of what had to be recognised and accepted as all the rest of nature. She only wished that she could participate in it. She heard no voices, received no visions, was given no instructions. Her madness had been nothing but empty anguish. There was no alternative reality for her. The god of Abram was cruel indeed.

She fetched clean water and cloths and set about bathing Abram's wound.

'This lord gives and takes away. In the old story, he created life, the first life, and told them to multiply. He paraded the rest of the world before Adam and told him to name them. Now, it seems, you are the new Adam. But this time he has taken back fertility and naming for himself. What is left to you?'

'Work and love.' Abram spoke with resignation. 'And pain.' He winced.

'Love? Isn't that his too? Doesn't he also demand love from you?'

'He does not understand human love. By default, it is ours. There is nothing I can do about the Lord, but there is nothing he can do about our love.'

'Do we still have love?'

'It is all we have, Sarah. Us is all we can have that can't be touched.'

'You've come to a strange wisdom, Abram.'

They sat on together in their tent in the world, close and quiet with each other, until the sun had set. Perhaps, after all, there could be both the madness and the way of the world. And if there was laughter, it might bridge the gap between Abram's longings and vision and Sarai's world of desert and necessity. The Lord could command, but Abram and Sarai could sit in silence and smile.

The following day Abram, host of the Orchard Hotel, sat in the entrance to his hospitality tent shaded by his pomegranate trees, nursing his wound, in the shimmering heat of the midday sun. Sarai lay in the cool interior sleeping lightly, easily roused by the sudden sound of Abram's voice. She raised herself from the cushion to see three men approaching along the heat-hazed road towards the tent, one, walking a little way in front of the other two, swathed in bright white. She heard Abram call out, 'Sir, please, rest with me a while under the trees. Have a little refreshment. Be my guest at our Orchard Hotel.'

Then he turned to the darkness of the tent. 'Sarah, we have guests, prepare a fine meal for the travellers.'

In pain, Abram rose to his feet and went towards them.

The man in bright white nodded and signalled to Abram to wait where he was. The men made themselves comfortable, but no one spoke during all the time the bread was baking and the lamb roasting. When the food arrived, they ate in silence.

'Where is Sarah?' the man asked, when they had done.

Sarai moved into the shadows by the entrance of the tent, to listen and look. He seemed, apart from his ability to shake off the dust of the desert, an ordinary enough man. Hardly all knowing, since he asked for her whereabouts, but she heard that he had asked for Sarah.

'She's inside the tent,' Abram said.

'Sarah will give birth to a son by you this time next year.'

Sarai gasped with rage at the impertinence of this stranger who mocked her ancient sterile body. Then, outraged, she began to laugh. 'How delightful,' she rasped through her laughter. 'Shrivelled with age, I am to become an object of desire to my equally shrivelled husband, and a breeder at last.'

The man turned towards her. He stared hard for a moment into the tent, without amusement, and returned his attention to Abram. 'Abraham, why does Sarah laugh at the idea that she will conceive? Is anything beyond the Lord? I will return in due time and you will have a son.'

Sarai stopped laughing and looked closely at the man who called them by the wrong names and promised in the name of Abram's lord. If this was one of Abram's visions, then she at last had been included, or at least permitted to be present. For a moment she was afraid. Not of the man, nor even of the power of the lord, but afraid that she might believe in the comfort offered by her inclusion, by that 'Is anything beyond the Lord?' And if she did, what would all her past life become? Hiatus, error, loss. She did not want to lose her life again, this time to belief, not even to assuage the misery or the emptiness. It was hers, her existence, she had lived it in the growing understanding that it was to be lived, that that was the point, the only point. She would not relinquish it to dreams of comfort. She stepped out of the shadow into the light and faced the man.

'I did not laugh,' she said, challenging him with her manifest lie.

'Yes, you did laugh,' the man replied, too insistently, and as Abram rose painfully to accompany the strangers on their way, she smiled a brittle smile at the man in bright white to let him know that, whoever and whatever he might be, still, she could choose ————

———— She knew who I was, but still she lied. Such a lie. 'I did not laugh,' when the sound of her mockery rang in the air. She meant 'I will not believe in you, no matter how you confront me with your reality.' What creatures are these, who can simply deny what presents itself to their senses? What power could I have in the face of flat denial? I gained a new understanding of my weakness. Abraham, after all the decades of promises and disappointment could choose to believe, and Sarah could choose to deny. And I was subject to their choices, I, their maker. If only they had known, they needed no child, they had one already, and not Ishmael. How strangely things had turned out. I could create and I could destroy, but I could not deny, or choose to believe or not believe, because *I am that I am* and I know what there is to be known. There was nothing, it seemed, that I could do about Sarah except destroy her, and now that Abraham had discovered how to laugh, what could I do but shake my power at him from time to time and give him what he wanted? These were, it seemed, my limitations. Endurance, denial and humour were my limitations. The world I had created was my limitation. As ever, it seemed, I had only the display of raw power.

Abraham and I walked towards the road that led to the cities of the plain. Sarah followed us at a distance, not knowing, perhaps not caring that I was well aware of her. Abraham, of course, had only ears and eyes for me. But the display I intended was not for him alone. If my murmured words of warning carried back on the breeze to the woman, so much the better ————————

———————— What is a poor human to do faced with raw power but invent justice? Call it whistling in the hurricane, but call it too the best we can do. Justice is just a numbers game, with a hastily invented set of rules that are forever ignored by one of the players. It is, in the end, as arbitrary as accident. But it is distinctively arbitrary, a recognisably human pomposity in the face of capricious oblivion. As the lord promised Abram a vivid example of what he could do to those who failed to please him, so Abram gave his lord a lesson in the nature of the creature he was threatening. The battle was incommensurate, to be sure, like a squeaky-voiced philosopher in the ring with the heavyweight champion of the universe, but Abram squeaked his novel idea and, for a moment, caught off-guard his lord of the heavy punches. What more can be done, except to refuse to enter the ring at all? Abram, in his longing and rage, had learned devious-ness, fancy footwork, but not refusal.

'Far be it from you,' he taxed his lord. 'Far be it from you to destroy the righteous along with the wicked.'

Sarai listened to her husband working his lord like a herdsman bargaining with a buyer at market, playing the numbers and value game for the lives of the inhabitants of Sodom and Gomorrah, her Abram who only the day before had butchered himself, slicing off his foreskin at the com-mand of his incorporeal lord, and she wondered not just at his faith but also at his self-belief. And then, of course, there was the sheer dumbfounding stupidity of it.

'What if there are fifty righteous folk among the wrong-doers? Will you destroy them for the sake of the bad ones?'

'If I find fifty good people, I'll spare the place for their sake.'

'Forty-five?'

'I'll spare it for forty-five.'

'Thirty?'

'I'll spare it for thirty.'

'Twenty?'

'I'll spare it for twenty.'

'Ten?'

'For ten,' said the visitor, whom Abram took to be his lord, turning away suddenly, and shaking the dust of the earth from his feet to make his getaway before the negotiations threatened parity between man and deity.

Perhaps, Sarai wondered on later occasions when she thought of this event, she had not been sleeping as lightly as she supposed inside the tent. Her recollection ended there, and memory put her once again in the darkness of the tent under the shade of the pomegranate trees. It didn't matter: the moment had redeemed something of *her* Abram, rebalanced him in her mind, so that the craven mess between his shaky old thighs, that enfeebling wish to be excused the reality of being human, was offset by a mind that reached for a way of being human, absurd perhaps, incommensurate certainly, hopeless without a doubt, but a stand, nevertheless, against the outrage of impotence. Abram invented justice out of the niggling of the human mind, something with which to reproach the arbitrary, to challenge it with a quality it could never conceive. Abram had begun the task of teaching the lord the nature of the humanity he was dealing with. Or in Sarai's dreams he had. Self-belief, stupidity, both, whatever it was, she was moved by him as she was moved, in spite of herself, by Ishmael's turbulent struggle with the world. To battle with the mind's wish for comfort was as much as could be expected of any creature. To risk the void, the emptiness, to reject the arms that threatened to enfold you, to draw you into the surrounding walls of love, was to begin a journey towards finding a way to exist in spite of the void. Sarai woke in the pomegranate orchard and found a heartbeat within herself, the passion for her brother, her husband, her fellow, that had withered but not after all died. After the waiting, love had returned.

Or else in Sarai's dreams it had. Perhaps the reflowering of love from the desert interior was simply herself spitting in the face of Abram's lord. Who knew better than she that it is easy enough to confuse wishes for reality, oneself for the other, solitude for solidarity? Even so, even if it were so, it was still a beginning. Her invention or Abram's, the notion of fairness took its place in the world and gave humanity something to fight omnipotence for. An idea took hold and stood against the anguish of inevitable failure.

Abram and Sarai stood together and wept in each other's arms in the following dawn, looking down at the cities of the plain gone up in smoke, humanity and its habitations erased by a force beyond control. Only Lot survived the end of that world, the marginal man, living always on the outskirts, never looking back. Only the last hope of the family of Shem, Lot and his daughters, remained to repopulate between them the devastated plains, the house of Shem for ever, it seemed, destined to turn in upon itself for its survival, while up in the hills, the old couple held each other firm against the shuddering aftershock beneath their feet ———————

——————— And here's the irony: it had come to the point where *I* needed the son of Abraham and Sarah. I had to ensure a continuation of their line, for what else was there for me in this unequal love between my Abraham and me? I needed the son, and the son of the son. I required the future, stuck as I was in eternity, while my merely fleshy beloved was doomed by the physics I had set in place to die. What would there be on earth for me if Abraham died without the son of my promise? I, too, was trapped in the way of the world. If Abraham had learned to be content with a contingent life, supported by Sarah, what would be left to me of my creation? All along, it turned out, my promises, my enticements to the human, had been promises to myself. How else could I ensure my continued presence on earth but by the continuation of Abraham's line? I longed to remain implicated, and I saw that humanity had the capacity to go its own way.

Now I feared abandonment. I knew the terror of bleakness, and eternity had become just that. I had created life, and in doing so, I had created loneliness. I could not bear not to love Abraham and the continuing fruits of Abraham.

And I knew, too (I'm not all sentiment) that there was only one way to separate the human pairing, Abraham and Sarah, as I saw them sustain each other against the worst I could do. Only a child, only a child between them could break the bond between them that kept me outside Abraham's heart. What they most wanted was the final weapon I had against them. A child who represented such different desires to each of them, and to me, was the only way to sever the love that held me at bay.

ENDING

*And it came to pass after these things, that God did tempt Abraham,
and said unto him, Abraham: and he said, Behold, here I am.*
GENESIS 22:1

Whoever the story belongs to, the events took place in
the world: in the world of wishes and dreams, perhaps, but
what more human a world could there be? If Abram's fear of
oblivion had caused him to invent this most personal and
interrupting lord of the narrative, his humanity had shown
that lord that there could be no commerce with the creator's
creation except by learning the trick of wishes and dreams.
We taught him a thing or two about being human. *I am that
I am* learned the power of *we would be*. We paid the price for
longing, but received in return a tenacity, in spite of all the
fallibility, all the subjection to the arbitrary. The lord of
Abram learned that we were not easy prey to our fantasies of
transcendence; that we invented and then resisted our own
dreams and wishes with all the perversity we could muster.
His story, her story, my story: it doesn't matter. The need to
tell it makes it a human story, whoever authors the narration.

Eternity needs nothing, humanity needs a story. And per-haps, after all, eternity is nothing without humanity interrupting it.

And Sarai, at last, quite out of the way of the world, con-ceived a child in her old age. Well, strange things happen. Cities disappear in storms of fire, shaken to destruction by the writhings of the earth. Mountains fall from the sky and blacken the sun. Rains fail to come or come in torrents that desiccate or wash the fields and habitations bare of all susten-ance. Men and women talk of love and blight each other's existence. Children are abandoned, children cry with fear and lie limp with hunger, children die. And Sarai and Abram had a boy whom they named Isaac, after the laughter that rises in the gorge once the weeping at these things has finally died away. It is all the way of the world.

The child was circumcised, it was true, but beyond that there was no mention of Abram's lord, no sacrifice sent up in thanks for a promise fulfilled. The child Isaac was new life to Sarai, another beginning that dissolved the life-long shadow that had encased her heart, and gave her back her long-lost stepmother, the half-loved half-sister, and the anonymous woman who began it all. And to Abram, Isaac was the promise of future. The family of Shem would remember its past in times to come when the son of Abram, and the son of the son of Abram, recited the begettings. Abram's name would echo in a world in which he had disintegrated into mere dust blown away; his existence would be reiterated in the speaking of his name. And Sarai, who cared, or thought she cared, for none of this, cradled new life in her arms, felt the warm damp breath against her breast, the sweet smell of a love created in the flesh, of a blank beloved life that grew further into the world and relationship with every passing day. She held what had been born out of the long, difficult labour of love between her and Abram, and it had life. It kicked and grasped and thrived and lived, lived, lived: this singular truth of Sarai and Abram, of their time, of the fact of them. Of us.

The lord of Abram's hopes and hopelessness was very nearly forgotten in this affirmation of holding together. The world took on a renewed importance. When Isaac was weaned, Abram held a great feast to celebrate his son in the world. Then they travelled again, this time a family of sub-stance, more a progress than desert wandering, while Abram consolidated his land, and claimed more, digging new wells, and making treaties so that his son could continue the task of making a nation whose people would number more than the stars in the sky or the sands of the desert. They settled at last in the west, in the land of the Philistines with whom a covenant of land rights was agreed, and there in the place of the well he had dug that he called Beer-sheba, Abram planted a grove of trees to shade the rest of their days, and as an afterthought dedicated it to his lord ————————

———————— And so we have at last this happy, human family. Ha! Humanity congratulating itself on the splendid achievement of being human. You will recollect the recent invention of human justice, so touching in its concern for life, for fairness. Oh, yes, they taught me a thing or two about good and evil, and human decency. 'Far be it from you that the righteous should be as the wicked. Far be it from you.' How touching. What sensitivity. What development. What drivel. Remember Hagar, the Egyptian child who moved even me to pity, though not to love? You hear no further mention of her in this story of heroic, embattled humanity struggling with eternity. What of her, and the wild lad who was Abraham's original son? What of those innocents entangled in the needs of the house of Shem? The not-so-satisfactory first fruit of Abraham's loins had remained a thorn in Sarah's flesh. Now that she had a child of her own – not the way of the world, but the wish of the Lord – Ishmael was an embarrassment. He was also a threat to Isaac. The wild boy teased the new child, laughed at his milksop nature, his mother's doting, his acquiescence to comfort and conformity even as a toddler, his willingness to allow himself to be immured in a solid wall of love. Ishmael played dangerous games with the lad. 'Just stand there with this pomegranate on your head, and I'll shoot it off with my arrow . . .' And then there were the looks he shot from under his black angry brow at young Isaac when he thought no one was watching. But Sarah was always watching. Yet the wild boy was human too, just as human as those who are so proud of their capacity to dream and invent the future conditional. He was one of theirs, just like those who thought so well of themselves, but he was inconvenient, not the pretty reflection they wished to see. And he was as he was, not because of me, or anything that I did or planned, but because of them, because he was born out of their distorted wishes, a temporary solution that grew knowing he had no real place in the world in which he had been engendered. A love-bereft child. They did not wish to see themselves in his dark, unhappy countenance. The humans made Ishmael, the troubled, fidgety lad with no place of his own.

And does the other narrator, so full of humanity's merits, mention that Sarah, seeing the surely righteous grievance in the eyes of Ishmael, sent him and his long-suffering mother away, into the desert? That she expelled them from their highly wrought civilisation? Or that Abraham, in his magnanimity, having at last found his quiet life, gave them a skin of water and a loaf of bread and pointed them towards the wilderness, where they foundered, the water gone, the bread eaten, and waited to die? Is that not part of the story, too? Such fine humanity. So moved by itself and its troubles. So dangerous to those who subvert their story of themselves.

Well, they were right. Ishmael, having been made what he was, was indeed a threat to Isaac, the pale, compliant child. And since I needed Isaac, the child of Abraham and Sarah, just as they did, I did nothing to stop the expulsion of Hagar and her boy. But I would not let them die. Even I would not do that. I struck a well for them, and made them sturdy in their desert surroundings. I turned Ishmael's wild, sharp eyes into those of a hunter, a survivor, hardened to the life of the wanderer. He, too, would become a great nation, this first son of Abraham. 'Let Ishmael thrive,' he had begged me, and I keep my promises.

Now, Abraham and Sarah had what they wanted. A

future, and a point to the past and present. And me, what of me? Did I have what I wanted, what, at the hands of the humanity that I had made, I had learned to want? Love? The love of my chosen one? The image of myself that I had set upon the earth? The only image I had created, it seemed, was their vision of themselves in me. I had learned to reflect them and their paltry human wishes. When I looked at them I saw myself longing with their longing, dreaming with their dreams. I needed Abraham's son just as Abraham needed him: to ensure a future for myself, because in the face of the fact of flesh and its inexplicable ways, eternity was not enough. I had been used to provide them with what they needed in order to justify their exist-ence, to bear their limitations, but what had I received in return? I wanted the love of my creation, I wanted proof that the world was mine, after all, now and ever shall be, world without end.

'Abraham,' I called, after so long a silence, his and mine.

'Here I am,' he answered quietly from the shade of his grove. No longer falling on his face in amazement or mirth. Just 'Here I am', as if his presence on earth was a separate fact from my existence. The time had come to test the truth of this ————

———— You begin a story, a telling, and by the end the story tells itself. Finally, motive, justification, character and meaning are futile. The end is reached, and by the end, none of it matters, because only the ending makes sense of anything that went before. Only a story without an end sustains the notion that the dreams and struggles of its protagonists account for more than the workings of chance and necessity. The only story without an end is one in which the narrator arrests the narrative. Happy endings, sad endings, inconclusive endings: nothing but artifice, just ways of stopping short. There is only and always just the one ending. The interruption is indeed the narrative.

Abram's dream was to create a story without an ending, but he did not have the strength to do without the authority of a dream narrator. Sarai took up the narrative, grasping the real nature of the story, but she did not have the strength to dream. Both were interrupted by what they called by different names, but which grew strong enough to call itself *I am* and make itself the way of the world, the end of all narration. In the end, it destroyed them, broke their love and their lives, but after all, it was only the way of the world that was made and remade by those who lived in it.

Sarai woke very early one morning to the end of her story. It was well before dawn, and she heard, in the distance, men talking in low tones in preparation for a journey. She picked out Abram and Isaac among the voices, and wondered lazily what excursion they might be making that they had not mentioned to her. Men's business, she thought, half asleep. A hunting trip; a father showing his son the extent of his territories, what would one day be his; a lesson for the lad in the nomadic life, a few days of hardship, away from the soft devotion of the women, so that a boy might learn to be a man. The men creep away in the early hours, leaving the women to sleep so that there will be no fussing and fretting. Sarai let them go. She would cherish the boy when he returned, exhausted and proud, no doubt, of managing to keep up with his father and the two other lads who went with them. Abram would come back pleased to have stripped some of the sweet boyishness away from his son, before returning him to his mother, whose anxiety for her child's well-being was understandable enough. God knew, she was hardly a weak woman, and she knew that Abram knew that whatever strength the boy had was from her at least as much as from him. But how she watched him, feasting her eyes on his growing limbs, how she enfolded him, this miraculous Isaac, who, after Sarai had spent so long a time in the barren wilderness confronting intractable matter, had at last come to her.

He was a quiet, considerate boy. A child of elderly parents whose carefulness with himself was as much concern for his mother and father as for his own interest. He knew the weight he had in their lives, had been told all his years how he was the child of promise, the son who had come long after all hope had gone. If a certain passivity resulted from his wish to live up to his promise, not to disappoint, it was understandable. He was content to permit his mother to encircle him with her arms and tell him stories about the way of the world, and his father to take him off and train him in the necessary skills of that world. He was pleased to do so, pleased to give so much pleasure to those who had waited so long for him and had surrounded him with their wall of love. Sarai lay back and allowed herself to finish the night's sleep, happy enough with the image of her husband and son, her Abram and her Isaac, striding together across the desert landscape ————

———— 'Take now thy son, thine only son Isaac, whom thou lovest, and get thee into the land of Moriah; and offer him there for a burnt offering upon one of the mountains which I will tell thee of.'

The man of few words said nothing. Not a muscle in his face moved as I demanded the death of his boy. What had I expected? I had confronted him before, and received his dumb silence in response. But this was surely worth a gasp, a plea, a cry for mercy. Nothing. He gave me nothing. The next morning he saddled up his asses and set out with a couple of lads and his precious son, well before dawn, well before Sarah was awake to ask the nature of the outing, and headed off in continued silence, in the direction of Moriah. He was implacable in his obedience, cruel in his refusal to rebel, just as I was implacable and cruel in my search for reassurance of his devotion. Who was mirroring whom, I cannot say. It hardly mattered any more. We had become each other's grim shadow.

'Father?'

'Here I am, my son.'

To me; now to the boy.

'Where is the sacrificial lamb?'

'The Lord will provide, my son.'

And not another word. They built the altar. He laid the

boy on it and tied him down. He covered the lad's eyes with
one hand and with the other raised the knife.

I knew everything I needed to know about the human. I
knew that neither he nor I would ever have love between us.
My will, my wish would never be enough. He tested me,
and found me wanting. I could not sacrifice the hope of
love, the future of love. I was not strong enough to exist
purely as will. I had created something else, desire, and I
could not risk an eternity of loss. I could only prove obedience. It was no longer enough. If I took the human future,
the dream, I would have nothing left for myself. Was
Abraham prepared to lose his dream to prove I could not
have his love, but only his obedience? Was there, indeed,
love at all, and not merely will? Had love been my invention,
after all?

I had been rendered too weak, too fearful, too human to
pass the test. I called out to him before the knife fell.

'Abraham, Abraham.'

'Here I am.'

And those were the last words he ever spoke to
me ————————

———————— There was to be a future. But that was all
there was to be. The past disintegrated, blown to fragments
by the wish and the fear. The fragments remained: this time
and that time, but they no longer cohered. They no longer
offered a story that made sense. Stories would be told – and
told and told – that were worked like shapeless clay or

lumpish stone into the semblance of sense, but the final form was always in the wishful eye of the shaper, never in the original material itself. The clay needed dreams and wishes breathed into it before it became anything recognisable. The present remained, but meant nothing, a bleak corridor, too dark to see ahead, too narrow to permit a backward glance. Sarai's heart was turned to stone by her final glimpse of the past before the ever-present darkness swallowed her up.

There never was such a silence as at the return of Abram and Isaac to the glade at Beer-sheba. Abram shut himself away in a room whose door remained closed to everyone. Isaac stood in front of his mother, a wraith, a pale, shivering ghost, transparent almost, like glass, and although he opened his mouth, no sound emerged. She laid him down in her bed and bathed away the beads of sweat that rolled down his face with cool water, and soothed his shaking body with her stroking hand. Finally, he slept, and when he woke, he told her in his new pale, ghostly voice of what had occurred on the mountain in Moriah.

And then there was a sound such as no one had heard ever before. People stopped what they were doing, stopped breathing even, as three long, languishing notes rang out and seemed to still the very air around Beer-sheba, so that the howl of loss that is the way of the world could be heard to the ends of the earth and at the very edges of time.

Then silence fell again like a weighty curtain and Sarai took herself away to Kiriath-arba in the land of Canaan, leaving the future behind her.

And here she lies on her bed and waits, while we keep

watch, while the tears slip down her ancient, expressionless face without any sudden surge of passion or obvious cause, as if the tears were welled already, brim full behind her shrunken eyes, and leak like spillage over the lids whose muscles are not strong enough to dam them up. She is waiting. That is all.

The Cure for Death by Lightening
Gail Anderson-Dargatz

'I loved it from the first page, she's fluent and graceful
and there's passion and tension – in fact, all I want
from a novel' – *Margaret Forster*

Beth Weeks is fifteen years old and lives with her parents
and rebellious older brother. Strange things are happening:
a classmate of Beth's is mauled to death; children go missing
on the nearby Indian reserve; and Beth herself is being
stalked by an indefinable force – shapeshifter? The mystifying
Coyote Jack? Turtle Valley is home to a host of eccentric but
familiar characters including Nora, a native girl in whose
friendship Beth takes refuge; Filthy Billy, who can't say a
clean sentence; and her own brooding father. Laced through
both the mystery and the daily farm chores are the recipes
and remedies that Beth's mother, Maud carefully records on
the vanilla-scented pages of her handmade scrapbook.

Now you can order superb titles directly from Virago

☐ The Things We Do to Make it Home   Beverly Gologorsky   £6.99
☐ The Cure for Death by Lightening   Gail Anderson-Dargatz   £6.99
☐ A Rough Guide to the Heart   Pam Houston   £7.99
☐ Man Crazy   Joyce Carol Oates   £7.99
☐ The Pleasing Hour   Lily King   £6.99

Please allow for postage and packing: **Free UK delivery.**
Europe: add 25% of retail price; Rest of World: 45% of retail price.

To order any of the above or any other Virago titles, please call our
credit card orderline or fill in this coupon and send/fax it to:

Virago, 250 Western Avenue, London, W3 6XZ, UK.
Fax 020 8324 5678   Telephone 020 8324 5516

☐ I enclose a UK bank cheque made payable to Virago for £ . . . .
☐ Please charge £ . . . . . . to my Access, Visa, Delta, Switch Card No.

Expiry Date ☐☐☐☐   Switch Issue No. ☐☐

NAME (Block letters please) . . . .

ADDRESS . . . .

Postcode . . . . Telephone . . . .

Signature . . . .

Please allow 28 days for delivery within the UK. Offer subject to price and availability.

Please do not send any further mailings from companies carefully selected by Virago ☐